GARDEN OF MYSTERY & INTRIGUE

VAMPIRES OF NEW ORLEANS
BOOK 2

Madalyn Rae

Cover Art by: JV Arts

I dedicate the second book of the "Vampires of New Orleans" series to Amelia. This wouldn't have been possible without her invading my dream and insisting that I write the first chapter of book 1.

For my dedicated readers! I couldn't do it without you.

bloodlust

YOU NEVER QUITE GET USED TO the smell of the French Quarter during Mardi Gras. It's a mixture of alcohol, urine, and other human excrements that I'd prefer not to think about at the moment. Being a vampire, my sense of smell is heightened to supernatural levels, which makes it even worse. I fight the urge to cover my nose as I walk past the unsuspecting humans, stumbling their way down Bourbon Street. Half of them have lost pieces of clothing in their attempt to receive more throws from the parades, most don't even realize it.

"Tell me again why we're here?" Viktor says as we dodge a large group of college kids.

"Edon asked me to keep an eye on Drew."

"Oh, yes. Now I remember...and why are we doing that?"

A large man, wearing a green sequin tiara, runs

directly into me, knocking me into the brick wall of a boarded-up store. "Watch it, asshole!"

"Bitch," the man mumbles and keeps walking.

"God, I hate this time of year." Viktor straightens his antiquated waistcoat and white shirt. "Want me to kill him?" he asks with a laugh.

"Nah, not tonight." I join in his laughter.

"If Edon asked you to attend to Drew, why am I here?"

"Because your immortal child of a daughter insisted you accompany me. She acts like I can't do anything on my own."

He huffs a laugh. "Agreed. She is a bit of a mother hen."

We dodge another large group of teens. "It's been almost a year since she changed me. I think it's time for her to give me a little freedom."

"You do realize you sound like a spoiled teenager, complaining about their parent?"

"I'm well aware of what I sound like, but you try having a thousand-year-old vampire, trapped in the body of a five-year-old for all eternity, be your maker. It's not an easy task." I stop in front of an inconspicuous bright red door. "This is it."

"Thank goodness. I was getting triggered by the crowd."

I can't control my laughter. "You've been on TikTok again, haven't you?"

"Maybe. How else am I supposed to become more hip?"

I look him up and down. "You can start by not dressing like you're straight out of a Jane Austen novel."

He looks down at his clothes. "I don't know what that means, but I'm guessing you're making fun of me."

"More like making a positive suggestion."

He makes a face. "Your positive suggestion can kiss my ass." The red door opens, revealing a large bearded man.

"What the hell do you two want?" The lycanthrope stares at us with hatred in his eyes.

"Edon sent me," I announce.

"Now, why would he do that?"

"Because they're going to play a game of cards. Are you going to let us in or block the entire door with your over-protective, pretentious puppy dog performance?" Viktor has the tact of a serial killer. "I'm growing quite bored."

The man grunts, opening the door wide enough for us to enter. "Drew's in the corner."

"Oh, look. You *do* know why we're here. Amazing how your memory magically started working again." The wolf glares at Viktor, who relishes the frustration he's causing.

"One day you're going to get us killed," I whisper as we head to the back corner.

"I would love to see him try," Viktor says loud enough for our door greeter to hear.

"Are you fucking kidding me?" Drew sets his beer on the table with a loud thud. "Edon sent two bloodsuckers to babysit me?"

"He's as excited as we are." Viktor slides into the side of the rounded bench. I slide in on the other side, turning the three of us into a werewolf sandwich. "Maybe you should use that pea-sized brain a little more, and you wouldn't need a *babysitter*."

"Whatever, vamp. I do what I want when I want. I don't care if you two are here or not."

"There was an overwhelming amount of w's in that sentence. Maybe tomorrow we can work on a new letter." Viktor is egging this guy on.

"Shut up, bloodsucker."

"My pleasure, puppy."

"Edon asked me to stay with you until the festivities of the night are over. Apparently, he's afraid you might do something to draw attention to the lycan. You want to share why he would think that?" I turn toward the large man, focusing on his eyes.

"Because he's an idiot," Drew answers.

"I'll be sure to relay that information to your alpha." Viktor pulls out his new cell phone, opening a familiar clock app. Up until a month ago, he insisted a cell phone was nothing more than "mindless entertainment for an idle mind." Although he's not wrong, I'm not sure what made him decide differently. He's quickly becoming one of the millions that are glued to their phone throughout the day.

Drew takes a swig from his beer bottle. "You look like that other vamp." I feel my eyes grow twice their normal size. I've kept the fact that I ran into Penelope at Opie's shop a secret. As far as I know, neither Viktor nor Celeste has any idea she's alive or dead. God, now that I'm a vampire, I should find out the answer to that question. Am I dead or alive? "She's way hotter, though."

"I'll keep that in mind." Looking around the room, I'm questioning why Edon decided I was the best person for this job. The room is full of drunk or passed-out lycan, sitting randomly around the room, while a small band plays jazz music. There's no wild partying going on, no dangerous interactions. In fact, this is the deadest Mardi Gras celebration I've ever seen. A few scantily clad women are walking around, trying to liven the party without much luck. "Are all lycan bars this exciting?"

Drew leans back, stretching his long legs in front of him. "No. This one is on the wild side."

Viktor laughs on the other side of him. "The comments are funnier than the videos." He continues swiping through his phone, ignoring my and Drew's conversation. I can't help the spontaneous rolling of my eyes.

"What does Edon think you're going to do?" I ask Drew for the second time.

He finishes his beer before answering. "He thinks

I'm going to turn into a wolf and wreak havoc on the city of New Orleans."

"Why would he think that?" Viktor asks, suddenly very attentive.

Drew sighs. "Because I don't want to do it anymore. I don't want to be stuck in this lifestyle. I want to be human."

I turn fully toward the wolf. "Human? Why?"

"Because I'm sick of this shit." He puts his hand in the air, ordering another drink. "I want to be in control of what I do and where I go, not be controlled by the wolf inside me." He takes a drink. "It's why Edon thinks I'm going to go rogue."

"Are you?" Viktor asks, looking up from his phone.

"No, I'm not an idiot. Unlike vamps, we work together as a group, as a pack." He sets his beer on the table. "That's why I did what I did."

Drew now has our full attention. "What did you do, Drew?" I ask, not sure I want to know.

"They should be here any minute." He takes another drink. Viktor makes eye contact with me.

"Who should be here?" he asks, looking around the smoke-filled room.

"I don't know *who* they are, just what they are." Viktor moves faster than the human or lycan eye can track. Within seconds, he has Drew backed into a corner and a hand across his neck.

"It seems you're not fully aware of who I am." Viktor has turned from an app-swiping robot into a killing machine in seconds. The rest of the wolves in the bar are watching, but none try to come to Drew's aid. "I'm going to ask that question one more time. *Who* should be here any moment?"

Drew struggles against Viktor's hold. "It's no use," I remind him. "Viktor is the strongest vampire in the city."

"I believe you mean the strongest vampire in the southern United States, my dear." Viktor doesn't release his hold on Drew's neck. "And my patience is running thin."

"They call themselves 'The Silver Bullets,'" Drew coughs out. "They take care of problems." On cue, the door to the bar slams open. The large wolf that was guarding the door is on the ground in a pool of blood within seconds. "They're here." Drew smiles. "My redemption is nigh."

Viktor releases Drew and moves toward the trio entering the bar. They're holding weapons and shooting randomly into the crowd. In the time it takes me to assess the scene, Viktor has already taken down two of the shooters and has the third one, a young woman, held tightly around the neck and her weapon on the ground. "Let me go!" she screams.

"Who are you?" he asks, inches away from her neck with fangs bared. I know he would never bite her, but she doesn't.

Her breathing picks up at the realization of what

has her in its grip. "We rid the world of filth!" she shouts over the roar of the bar.

Viktor's voice is low and calculated. "I don't believe that answered my question. We're going to try that once more. "Who are you?" Instinctually, I move in front of the girl, and for the first time since becoming a vampire, I copy Viktor's lead and bare my fangs. The girl screams.

"I believe my friend asked you a question," I spew.

"Meredith...my name's Meredith."

"Who sent you?" Viktor asks from behind, refusing to let go of her neck.

Meredith is breathing hard. "God sent me." Without warning, the girl slices her throat with a knife neither of us saw her holding. Her scared face changes to a smile as she collapses on the floor in a thud of blood.

Since becoming a vampire, I've never drunk human blood, and that's the way I want it to stay. I've drank nothing but goat's blood since day one. However, being surrounded by this much blood is more than I can handle. Something inside me begs to drain the blood remaining in the girl's body.

"Amelia, look at me." Viktor's voice is nothing more than an echo in the shadows of my mind. The blood calls to me, beckoning me toward it. "Amelia!" his voice whispers, not able to break the barrier of the bloodlust. In an instant, I'm on top of the girl and drinking from her neck. The warmth of the blood meets a need I didn't know was there. Her blood rushes through my body, making me sigh with relief. In an instant, I'm ripped away from the comfort of her blood and into the sky high above the festivities. Drinking human blood makes me feel more alive than I've ever felt. I want more, I *need* more.

Minutes later, I'm in the living room of the house in Mandeville and lying on the couch. "What happened?" my maker asks, running into the room.

"She had human blood," Viktor answers.

"She wasn't ready. This is why I didn't want her to go out." Everything in the room feels alive. Small pinpricks cover my skin, and the energy that surrounds me is intoxicating. I want more blood. I *need* more blood.

"More!" I scream, moving to stand. I need to get back to that bar, to the girl, while her blood is still fresh. Celeste is on me in an instant, pushing me back on the couch.

"How did she get human blood?" she asks through the blood-induced fog that's filling my brain.

"It's a long story. Let's get her into her room. She's going to have to detox." Viktor picks me up, carrying me up the stairs. The feeling floating through my head reminds me of the first time I got drunk. The sound of giggling echoes through my ears as I'm being carried.

"Why is she giggling?" Celeste asks.

"Because she's drunk," Viktor answers, opening the

door to my room. "She'll be better in the morning, but she's going to have a pretty bad hangover."

I hear my tiny maker sigh deeply as I'm placed on the bed. The side of the bed indents as Celeste climbs beside me. "Amelia, get some rest. You'll feel better tomorrow. Next time you want to leave, I'm going with you."

I hear Viktor laugh in the background as the door clicks shut. The haint blue ceiling fades into nothing as I sink into the blackness of bliss.

TWO

stranger from mississippi

MY HEAD FEELS like an elephant took up residence while I slept. I've been drunk many times in my life, but this is the worst hangover I've ever experienced. The overwhelming hunger rumbling through my body is almost more than I can handle. The door to my room creaks open. "Amelia?" I recognize the voice of my tiny maker. "Are you awake?"

"No," I whisper. "I feel like poop."

Celeste laughs at my word choice. "Daddy says you're going to feel horrible for a while. You have to detox off the blood."

"What does that mean?"

"It means you're going to feel like poop for a few more days." She hands me a glass of red liquid she had hidden behind her back. "I brought you breakfast."

I know without asking, it's goat's blood and not what my body craves. "Thank you, Celeste."

"What happened last night?" she asks.

My mind flashes back to the scene and the blood-shed at the bar. "To be honest, I don't know. Where's Viktor?"

"After he brought you home, he went back to the city. He should be back soon." I sit up in bed with a realization that just now hit me.

"Celeste, I slept. I haven't slept since the change, but I slept after having the blood."

She laughs. "You didn't sleep. You were passed out. The first time a vampire drinks human blood can be overwhelming." She looks down with her words.

"Do you want to talk about it?" I can tell there's more on her mind than my passing out drunk. No doubt, she's remembering her own change and life afterward.

"Nope," she says, sliding off the bed. "Rest and when you stop feeling like poop, come downstairs." She giggles, leaving my room.

I don't know how much time passes, but eventually, my head begins to feel well enough to get out of bed. I take a long shower, washing any remnants of the bar from my body. An hour later, I'm dressed and heading downstairs.

"There she is," Viktor announces as I hit the last step. "Looks like you survived the bloodlust."

"I still have a massive headache, but the elephant has taken up residence somewhere else."

"I don't know what that means," he admits. He closes a laptop, sliding it onto the table beside him.

"Are you using computers now?"

"It's important to evolve with the times, and yes, I'm using a laptop. I've been researching 'The Silver Bullets,' and the Google is much more productive than any physical way I've found. Look at this." He motions me over, opening the laptop again. "This is their website."

"You're on the dark web? I know *the* Google didn't take you there easily."

"What's the dark web?"

"Never mind. What did you find?" I stare at the ancient vampire who's somehow managed to go from never using modern electronic devices to finding his way into the dark web overnight.

"It seems they've been around for the past twenty years. They operate under the pretense of a religious organization and are led by this man." He clicks on a picture of a middle-aged man. He's overweight with greasy hair and missing teeth.

"Gregory Stephens?" I read the label under his picture. "He's hot. Who is he?"

Viktor laughs. "From what I've researched, he's their leader." He clicks on another link, opening up another page. "Read this."

"Mission statement," I read out loud. "The Silver Bullets are a group who operate around the southern United States. Our mission is to rid the world of the filth that fills our streets and corrupts our young. Death is their freedom." He clicks on a few more pages, revealing pictures of scenes similar to the bar. "Holy shit. These people are crazy."

"It appears so."

"What do we do about it?" I ask, taking the laptop from him.

"*We're* not going to do anything." I continue flipping through pages of similar pictures.

"Do you think Edon knows about them?"

"That's a question for him. You can ask him when he gets here." I look up in a startle.

"He's coming here?"

"He is, and he's bringing someone with him."

I close the laptop. "Are you sure that's a good idea? I'm still on a human blood hangover. Is exposing me to more opportunities to feed the smartest idea right now?"

"He's bringing a vampire."

"What's to keep me from attacking Edon and eating him?" I ask a serious question.

"Me." Viktor smiles as the doorbell rings. I swear he planned this conversation at the perfect time.

Fran is at the door before either of us can get to it. She opens it, revealing two men. Standing next to the lycanthrope alpha is a man I don't recognize. He's nearly as tall as Edon. His hair is a dirty blonde color and sweeps to the side of his face. A perfectly formed jawline and deep blue eyes stare into my soul. "Welcome, gentlemen." Viktor motions toward the seating area in the front of the house. "Please, have a seat." Both men follow directions.

"Would either of you care for something to drink?" Fran asks, moving into the room.

"I'm good, thank you," Edon answers.

"I'd love some goat blood," the blonde vampire answers. Fran disappears and returns minutes later, holding a bottle of red liquid. I watch as he drinks the blood in one gulp. "That was perfect, thank you." He has an accent that reminds me of Jamie Fraser, making me instantly intrigued, and I envision him wearing a kilt.

"What happened last night?" Edon asks, interrupting my happy thoughts.

"A group came into the bar and started shooting," Viktor answers. "I've done some research. It seems they've been around for the past twenty years and are some sort of vigilante group, set on ridding the world of the filth that fills the streets. They've just now made their way into New Orleans."

The new vampire laughs. "You'd think they would've started here."

"They didn't seem like the sharpest pencils in the box," I answer.

"I'm sorry, I don't know your name." He stands, moving in front of me.

"Amelia Lockhart." I reach my hand out to shake his, but instead, he takes it into his, kissing the back of my hand, sending shivers up my spine. Why did I like that?

"Oliver Fitzgerald, but my friends call me Ollie," he whispers onto the skin covering my hand, causing goosebumps to form instantly.

"Mr. Luquire." He turns toward Viktor. "I'm here from Natchez, Mississippi." He steps away from my hand.

Viktor stares at the new vampire. "Why is that any of my concern, Mr. Fitzgerald?"

"Because we've seen the same thing in our city."

"If you were aware of this organization being in other cities, my question is, why would you send Amelia into a situation that could turn out to be similar?" Viktor sounds angry as he approaches the alpha. "If I hadn't been with her, she might not have survived."

Edon looks down. "I can assure you it wasn't on purpose. I felt something was wrong with Drew, but nothing to this magnitude, and never put the two issues together as one. I would never put her in harm's way." He turns to me. "Amelia, I'm truly sorry to put you in that predicament."

"It's fi..."

"No, it's not fine," Viktor interrupts. "Do your research next time." I haven't seen this side of Viktor since I was held captive in his home. He's in predator mode and making sure his point gets across. I look between the two of them, not sure what to say.

"Understood," Edon answers.

"What makes you think the group that attacked the bar last night is the same group that's been in Natchez?"

"We don't," Oliver answers.

"Then why are you here?" Viktor doesn't mince words. "You should be talking to your wolf, Drew. He knew who they were and had been in contact with them."

"I have. He's in isolation for the foreseeable future." I don't want to know what isolation could possibly mean. I picture Drew sitting in a locked room, alone with his thoughts.

"To answer your question, sir, I am here because not only have they been attacking lycan, they've been attacking and killing vampires as well." That grabs Viktor's attention. "The attacks are not just in Natchez. There have been reports as far north as Tupelo and as far south as Biloxi."

"What does this mean?" I ask the men sitting in front of me.

"It suggests this group is bigger than their website suggests," Viktor answers.

"We've found research that led us to New Orleans and have reason to believe their leader has moved here and is working with a vampire from the city."

"That makes no sense," I argue. "If they're working with a vampire, why would they be killing them?"

"Because the vampire they're working with is

ancient and powerful and seems to have an agenda," Ollie answers.

"Are you saying there's another ancient vampire in New Orleans?" Viktor asks.

"Aye."

"See, that's where you're wrong. I'm the oldest vampire in New Orleans. Unless you know something I don't, you may leave." Viktor's dislike for Oliver is obvious.

Edon leads the duo toward the door. "We'll be in touch when we discover more information." He stops at the door. "Amelia, I'm truly sorry." I move in front of him and wrap my arms around his waist.

"I know. I'm fine."

"It was a pleasure to meet you, Miss Lockhart." Oliver takes my hand in his and kisses it once more before following Edon out the door.

"Well, that was interesting." Viktor claps his hands loudly after the door is closed.

"Do you think there's another ancient in the city?" Celeste comes down the stairs.

"You've been eavesdropping again, mon petit amor."

"You know, technically, I'm older than you. You're not the oldest or the strongest." She smirks.

"Yes, but that's our little secret." Viktor picks her up, pulling her close. I watch the two of them and guilt hits me straight in the heart.

"I need to tell you both something." The duo turns

to me with confused looks on their faces. "You might want to sit down."

"Go upstairs, Celeste," Viktor demands.

"No, this involves her, too." Celeste sits next to me, wrapping her tiny arm through mine.

"Why do I get the sense this is not going to be news I'm going to enjoy?" he asks, remaining standing.

"Celeste, do you remember the first time I went into the city alone? The day I turned in my thesis?" She nods. "I didn't go straight to the university and back. I made a quick stop." I pause before continuing. "I stopped at Opie's shop off the square."

"The witch?" Viktor asks.

"Yes. I don't know why I stopped, other than I just wanted a little bit of normalcy back in my life. When I walked in, she wasn't alone. There was another person in the back with her. It was a woman, and she was demanding Opie make her some sort of spell."

"You think this woman was an ancient vampire?" Viktor interrupts.

"She threatened Opie if the spell wasn't done quickly, and I could tell from the tone of her voice, Opie was scared. When I turned, I saw who the woman was." I sigh, not sure how to blurt out that Viktor's wife, Celeste's mother, isn't dead. "She looked identical to me."

"What are you saying?" Viktor moves closer to me. "This isn't a joke, Amelia."

"I'm not joking, Viktor. The woman had long red curls and bright blue eyes."

"Daddy?"

"Go upstairs, now," Viktor demands of his daughter. Celeste sighs but follows directions. He waits until she's out of earshot before speaking. "Is this some sort of joke to you? I opened my home to you, and you pull a stunt like this?"

"I'm telling you the truth. It was Penelope, and she spoke to me."

"If this happened six months ago, why bring it up now?"

"Because I knew how it would affect the two of you." I move toward him.

"No, stay where you are. Saying something like that to me is one thing, but saying it in front of my child is another." Anger pours off of him. He moves to the other side of the room in a flash. "Celeste and I will be leaving tonight. Don't look for us." He disappears in front of my eyes, leaving me alone and dumbfounded. What the hell just happened?

THREE

harrison knew...

TRUE TO HIS WORD, the house is nothing more than an empty shell. What do I do? Should I pine over the fact that I'm alone and have no idea where to get the goat blood? My stomach growls at the thought. God, I'm helpless. When did that happen? I pull out my phone and text the only person I know who can help.

> Hey, Violet! Whatcha doing?

> Amelia?

> Yep! I haven't talked to you in a while, I miss you.

> Girl, we haven't talked in six months.

God, I'm a horrible friend.

> Yeah, I'm sorry about that. Would you like to meet up tonight?

Violet doesn't answer right away, and I decide she's not going to. An hour later, I'm heading across the lake and into the city. My phone buzzes, drawing me back to the reality of the situation.

> Sure! How about Café du Monde?

> Coming into the city now. I'll meet you there in thirty minutes.

Exactly thirty minutes later, I'm sitting in the middle of tourists covered in powdered sugar. Thankfully, the bloodlust has left, and I have no desire to eat one of them. Out of nowhere, Violet sits at the empty seat at my table. I didn't hear or sense her arrival. "Thank you for coming." I smile at my one and only friend.

"Of course!" She reaches over, hugging me. Her hair is bright purple and sticks out stylishly all over her head. She's wearing a black leather coat, skin-tight blue jeans, and three-inch patent leather heels. I changed into a pair of jeans and a sweater before leaving the house, but compared to Violet, I look like I buy my clothes at a secondhand shop. "How's life with Viktor?"

"It's good," I lie. "Nothing super exciting. How about you?"

"Good. The house gets lonely. If you ever want to

get away from Viktor for a few days, feel free to come and stay. Although, I'm not sure your mini maker would allow it." I laugh, awkwardly. "How is Celeste, anyway?"

"Other than being my mother, she's fine. She's a great kid, and we've grown really close." I fight to keep the sadness from sounding through my voice.

"Are you going to tell me what's going on?" she asks.

"What do you mean?" I take a sip from the coffee I ordered when I arrived. It's cold and tastes like ass.

"I mean, something's up. Not that I don't love hearing from you, but you're here alone, no babysitter or anything." She looks around at the tourists. "Celeste would never allow this."

Is it that obvious?

"Viktor's a little angry at me right now. He and Celeste left."

She leans back in her chair. "This is the kind of gossip I live for. I'm all ears." I give her the shortened version of everything, starting with the Mardi Gras vigilantes and ending with Viktor taking Celeste and leaving. "So, who was this Oliver dude?"

"Out of everything I just told you, you're stuck on Ollie?"

"He sounds kind of hot." Her words bring a well-needed laugh.

"Now that you mention it, he was pretty hot."

Violet stands, pushing her chair under. "Why don't

you come to the house tonight? You won't have to drive back across the lake, and I could use the company. Maybe we could go shopping tomorrow. You know, for old time's sake."

"Honestly, that sounds great." I push my chair under the table and follow her to the street. Her red BMW is parked next to the one Celeste bought me. "I'll meet you there."

I don't attempt to keep up with her driving as she weaves in and out of traffic. By the time I turn the corner to the garage, I figure she's been inside for at least ten minutes.

I pull into the garage, surprised to find what was once full of cars, only holding a few. One of which is my twenty-year-old Nissan, completely repaired and looking beautiful. "Violet?" I call into the empty kitchen as I enter. Being back in this house brings back memories I'd rather forget.

"In here," she answers from the sitting room. The house looks just like I remember. She hasn't changed anything in the year since I've been here.

"The house looks great," I say with a smile.

"No, it doesn't. It looks like Harrison decorated it. I need to put my spin on it but haven't had the desire. Although," she opens the door to what was Harrison's office, "I did do something in here."

Instead of the oversized desk and bookshelves that once occupied the room, it's been turned into a small movie theater. A large screen hangs where the once floor-to-ceiling bookshelves sat, and a row of theater seating is perched in front.

"Oh, my God. This is great!"

"I know, right? Pick out a movie, and I'll go change." She points to a closet on the left side of the screen. The inside of the small closet looks like a Blockbuster Video threw up inside, and to my OCD joy, they're alphabetized by genre. I scan through each shelf, unsure what I'm in the mood for. In the past year, I haven't seen a television, let alone a movie. I choose one of my favorites and bring it to the theater chairs with me. Violet pops back in the room, wearing fuzzy pajamas and a long-sleeved sweatshirt.

"What did you choose?" I hand her the box, hoping she won't argue. "Oh, this is one of my favorites." She sticks the disc in, and the room comes to life. "I have nine speakers spread throughout the room and in the seats. If you can't hear the movie, you have a hearing problem."

I laugh as the opening scene of *Pride and Prejudice* comes on screen. Halfway through the movie, I'm in tears, and Violet is on her phone. This has always been one of my favorite books, and the movie is almost as good. My phone buzzes, drawing me out of my Jane Austen coma.

I miss you.

I stare at my phone, not sure who sent me a text.

> Who is this?

> Are you being safe?

In an instant, I know Celeste is the one texting me. I have no clue when she got a phone.

> I'm being safe. Pinky promise. I miss you, too.

> I'm talking sense into Daddy. I know you weren't lying.

"Amelia? Are you sure you saw Penelope?" Violet's words draw me away from my phone.

"One hundred percent."

"If she's alive, does that mean Harrison was innocent?"

I turn toward Violet. "He may have been innocent of killing Penelope, but he definitely wasn't innocent. He nearly killed me, and who knows how many he's killed over the years. If it weren't for you, I would've been another one of his victims."

She stares at the screen in silence. "I was one of his victims. I didn't want to become a vampire."

"What?"

"When he made me, he did it because *he* wanted to, not because I wanted it."

"That's not what he..."

"Not what he told you?" she interrupts. "That

doesn't surprise me at all." She looks down, fidgeting with her fingernails. "He followed me to the café, the same one where we met." I nod, remembering him saying the same. "I was with some friends, and we were out celebrating my friend's upcoming wedding. He found us, turned on the charm, and I fell for it hook, line, and sinker." She pauses, deep in memory.

"I was young and foolish. I'd never been with a man before and fell hard for his game. He tricked me into leaving with him and leaving my friends behind. They all encouraged me, thinking I was the luckiest girl in the world. Little did they know my life as I knew it would soon be over." She picks at her bright red finger-nail. "He left me for dead on the banks of the river. I remember watching him walk away. I was unable to speak and barely breathing, waiting for death to find me. I don't know what made him come back, but he did. It could have been a minute later, an hour later, or a day later. I don't know. I remember he was surprised to find my body still there and that I was alive. Whether out of kindness or cruelty, I'll never know. He drained the rest of my blood after forcing me to drink from him and turning me...into this. It was my fault. I should've stayed with my friends instead of going with him."

"No, it's not your fault, Violet. You can't blame yourself for something you had no control over. You were just another victim of Harrison's lies. He had no right to take your life away from you."

"It's why I wouldn't turn Thomas without his

permission. I won't do that to another person. I won't take someone else's choice away from them."

"I'm so sorry. I know what that feels like." I think back to the night Celeste turned me. I had no choice, but without her, I would've died. Am I angry that my choice was taken from me? Honestly, I've never thought about it before.

"Yeah, I guess you do." She sets her hand on top of mine, wiping a tear. "Your room is still set up from when you were here. In fact, your clothes are still in the closet. Feel free to stay as long as you like. I'm glad you texted me." She gets up, leaving me alone in the room.

How could I have been so dumb? I believed everything Harrison told me, every story, every lie, without question. When he told me the story of Violet becoming a vampire, he made it sound like he was her hero. "Asshole," I say out loud before heading upstairs.

Violet was right. The room is just as I remember. What once felt like a safe place, a sanctuary, now holds a completely new energy. I head up another flight of stairs to Harrison's room. The bed where we made love is sitting untouched as are the pictures covering the fireplace mantle and table.

I pick up the picture of Celeste. "How could your mom leave you like that?" I rub my fingers along her tight curls, bringing a smile to my face. Picking up the picture of Penelope, I study her features. We look so much alike, it's creepy. "You're a bitch and a bad mom." I look back at the king-sized bed. Something inside of me clicks, and I pull the covers off the perfectly made bed.

Without thinking, I jump on top of the mattress, running clawed fingers through the puffy mattress topping. Goose feathers and foam fly throughout the room. Once destroyed, I jump off the bed, looking for something else. The large wardrobe is the first thing I see. I rip the door off the hinges, pulling out what remains of Harrison's clothing. I meticulously rip the sleeves off of each shirt, tear each button from its home and separate each seam of his perfectly tailored closet. I turn, looking for more when I see Violet standing in the doorframe.

"Having fun?" she asks with a smirk.

"Actually, I am. You should join me." She moves into the room, stepping in front of a tall chest of drawers and carefully opens one of the drawers.

"God, I hated this shirt." She pulls out a brown and orange paisley shirt that looks straight out of the '80s. Putting both hands on the collar, she pulls, tearing the shirt into two pieces. "Oh, you were right. This is fun!" She does the same with every item in the chest of drawers. We turn, facing the only untouched piece of furniture in the room, a small stand next to the bed.

"Shall we?" I ask, moving to the cabinet. I pull out the drawers, setting them on what remains of the mattress. We each take one and begin shredding the papers that fill each one. The freedom of watching Harrison's belongings be destroyed is what the two of us needed. I look around the once spotlessly clean room and take a deep breath. "God, that felt good."

"Yes, it did," Violet agrees, picking one of the empty drawers off the floor. "I should've done this a year ago." She looks me in the eye, tears filling her eyes. "Thank you, Amelia."

"I'm glad my spontaneous anger helped both of us." My words make her laugh, and the two of us sound like cackling hens for the next few minutes. She sets the drawer she's holding upside down on top of the chest, and it makes a strange clicking sound. "What was that?" I ask, righting the drawer. A false bottom falls to the floor, followed by a manilla envelope.

"What do you have hidden in here, dear Harrison?" Violet picks up the envelope, ripping the top open. "Oops." She laughs. Her face turns serious. "Amelia, look at this." She clears an area of the floor and dumps the contents. Several photographs, a flash drive, and newspaper clippings are on the floor.

"What the hell is this?" I ask, picking up the photographs.

"Is that you?" Violet asks, taking the picture from me.

"I...I don't think so. I don't own any clothes like that." She turns the picture over, looking for any clues.

"Here's another one." She picks through the photographs, finding another picture of what looks like me, but wearing clothes I've never owned. "Is this

Penelope?" she asks, scattering the images around on the floor.

"It has to be. Did Harrison know she was still alive?"

"From the looks of it, yes." Violet opens one of the newspaper articles and reads the headline out loud. *"Local Biker Bar Destroyed After Fire Sweeps Through, Killing 14."* She picks up another article and reads it. *"10 Dead During Shooting Spree at Local Bar."*

"What are these?" I sort through at least a dozen more of the same.

Violet picks up the flash drive. "Let's see what's on this." I follow her to her room and laptop. She slides the drive into her computer, pulling up an encrypted page. "Shit. We need a password."

"Try asshole." She laughs but doesn't type it in.

"It's encrypted. Trying too many wrong passwords will lock us out permanently."

"I need to talk to Viktor." We head back into Harrison's room, stuffing the contents back into the envelope.

"I'm coming with you," Violet says, following me out of the door. "Do you know where to find him?"

"Good question." I pull my phone out, finding the last number that texted.

> I found something that Viktor needs to see.

My phone buzzes back instantly.

Is it about Penelope?

Yes.

A location marker pops up on my phone. Celeste sent me a damn location marker on her phone. The same girl who had never watched a movie knows how to send a location marker.

On our way.

FOUR

disguises are disgusting

THIRTY MINUTES LATER, Violet and I pull in front of a modern brick home in a small neighborhood on the outskirts of the city. "Viktor has a house in the suburbs?" Violet laughs at the scene. A minivan sits in the driveway, and a few toys are scattered in the yard. "Are you sure this is the address?"

"According to the location marker Celeste sent, this is it."

"I never had Viktor pegged as the soccer mom type." We step out of the SUV and head across the grass. Neither of us knows what to do once we get to the door. "Do we knock?"

I shrug, pushing the doorbell button next to the door. "Shit," a voice on the other side of the door says. The door cracks open, and Fran sticks her head outside. "Hello, ladies."

The door swings wide, and Celeste comes running

outside. "Amelia!" She wraps her arms around my waist, pulling me tight. "I knew you'd find us. I missed you."

"I missed you, too. I don't think your dad is going to be as happy to see me as you are."

"Aww, he'll get over it. Come in." We follow her, finding the inside very much like the outside. The foyer leads into an open living room and dining room combination and looks like a typical middle-class suburban family home.

"Where is Viktor?" Violet asks.

"Mr. Luquire has gone to the city. Can I get you something to drink?" Fran asks.

"Actually, I would like that, thank you." She disappears, returning moments later with a glass of red liquid. I drink the entire glass, calming my rumbling stomach.

"Want to play a game?" Celeste asks. "I don't have as many games here, but I have some playing cards. We could play GO FISH."

"That sounds great. Can Violet play, too?"

"Of course!" Celeste sits on the floor and starts dealing the deck of cards. She manages to beat both of us four times before the front door opens. For the first time since I've known her, she looks nervous. "Don't tell Daddy how you knew where to find us." I nod, understanding.

"Why are you here?" Viktor stands in the doorway

with his arms crossed over his chest. Celeste squeezes my hand, offering strength.

I clear my throat before speaking. "Violet and I found something." I move in front of him, handing him the envelope. He ignores my offering and continues staring into my soul. Heat rises in my cheeks, and I lower my hand. "Look, I know you're angry, and I don't blame you. I know how much Penelope meant to you, but trust me when I say, I would never use that knowledge against you." I look at my tiny maker. "I would never do that to her. Look through the envelope."

Viktor's face softens as he pulls the envelope from my hand and opens it. He flips through the photographs and newspaper clippings without saying a word, stuffs them back in the envelope, and hands it back. "Is there anything else?"

"Viktor, did you look at them?"

"Yes. I saw you dressed in different clothing and in different areas around the city."

I knock the envelope to the floor. "Dammit, Viktor. Those aren't pictures of me. I don't own those clothes, and I've never been in those locations."

"Did you read the clippings?" Violet asks, coming to my side.

"I don't know what you're trying to do or how to make it any clearer." He sighs, showing his teeth. "Leave me and my daughter alone. You are not welcome here."

"Daddy?" I turn, seeing Celeste holding the photographs from the envelope.

"Celeste, those are not pictures of your mother. It's some kind of inappropriate joke that Amelia is playing on us." His voice is softer when he speaks to her.

"Look," she says, pointing to a small scar next to the woman's eye in the picture. "Harrison did that to her before he...before he changed us." She looks up at me. "Amelia doesn't have a scar." Viktor takes the picture from Celeste's hands, studying the small mark before moving in front of me and searching for the scar. "See, Daddy. These aren't pictures of Amelia." She hands him another photograph. In this one, the scar is clearly visible. He looks at me once more for confirmation.

Viktor moves to a chair, sitting down heavily. "Celeste, go outside and play with Fran."

"But, Daddy..."

"Go," he demands.

"Come, child. I'll let you chase me around the backyard." Fran ushers her through the back door.

"Where did you get these?"

"We found them at my house, in Harrison's room," Violet answers.

He looks through the photos once more. "Is this her? Is it Penelope?"

"I think so," I answer. "It's the same woman I saw at Opie's store. There's no other explanation."

"Do you realize what this means?" His voice is sad. I don't answer. He stands, moving across the room. "It means she didn't leave us because Harrison killed her. It means it was her choice to leave, her choice to leave her child." Pain sounds through his words. "What kind of a person does that? What kind of mother does that?"

"I don't claim to know why she did what she did, but I think there's more to the story than her being alive." I hand him the newspaper clippings. He reads through them, not sure what I'm trying to tell him. "I think these are related to 'The Silver Bullets,' and I'm guessing that Penelope is the ancient who's been helping them."

"This is getting better by the minute."

"There was something else," Violet says, pulling the flash drive from her pocket.

"I don't know what that is," Viktor admits.

"It's a flash drive, but it's encrypted." He stares at her with a blank look. "It has to have a password to see what's on it, and I don't know what the password is. If I enter the wrong password too many times, it will lock up permanently."

"What do you think is on it?" he asks.

"From the contents of the envelope, it looks like Harrison discovered Penelope was alive and was working on connecting the pieces together."

"I can decipher the encryption," Celeste says from another room. I turn, spying my maker peeking around the doorframe. "I took several classes on encryption. I should be able to figure it out."

"So much for being outside." Viktor crosses his arms.

"Oh, I was outside. I just came in for a drink of water," Celeste lies.

"Vampires don't drink water," Viktor reminds her.

She sighs. "Okay, I was eavesdropping. That's not the point here. I can do it. I can figure out the encryption. Let me try." Viktor reluctantly hands her the flash drive. She runs to the corner of the room, pulling a laptop out of her backpack. "Got it," she announces several minutes later.

"Seriously," Violet asks, moving closer to the screen. "What is it?"

"It looks like a series of photographs." She clicks on a few of the files, pulling up a photo of Penelope outside Opie's store.

"There's a document on here." The file opens, covering the screen. "It's some kind of bank record of something called 'The Silver Bullets.' According to this, they have a benefactor that's been feeding millions of dollars into their account."

"More like filtering," Violet says. "Probably some kind of front for something worse."

"Are you sure about this?" Viktor asks the mini genius.

"Yep." She closes her laptop and jumps off the couch. "I'm going outside now. Let me know when it's time to go home." Celeste heads outside.

"Amelia, I'm sorry I didn't believe you." Viktor

makes eye contact with me. "I should've trusted you more, and for that, I apologize."

"Apology accepted," I answer. "The question is, what do we do with this knowledge?"

"We find the bitch," Violet answers. Viktor looks down at her choice of words, and I shoot her a look. She shrugs.

"We need to meet with Edon and Oliver." Viktor stands. "We'll follow you back to Mandeville. I'll contact them on the way and have them meet us there."

......

It doesn't take long before we all return to the Mandeville house. Celeste is running through each room, acting like it's been years since she's been here. When she's not running around, she's practically glued to my side. Since we've been back, she hasn't mentioned anything about Penelope, and honestly, I'm surprised after seeing the photographs. She's lived the past several hundred years believing her mother is dead, only to find out she's alive and living in the same city she is. I'm not a mother, but I can guarantee I would never allow my child to think I was dead. Edon and Oliver arrive not long after we do. I catch Violet checking Ollie out as the two of them find a place to sit. She's right. He is rather hot.

"Good afternoon, Miss Lockhart," Ollie says, kissing the back of my hand.

"Hello, Mr. Fitzgerald," I return. "It's a pleasure to see you again." I'm not sure why I sound so formal. When did that happen?

"Please, call me Ollie," he reminds me.

Viktor clears his throat, interrupting whatever's going on. "Amelia and Violet found this at Chamberlin's house." He throws the envelope on a table in the middle of the group. Edon is the first to take it, flipping through the contents.

"Is this you?" he asks me.

I shake my head. "Nope."

"Then who the hell is it?"

"Penelope," Viktor answers.

"*The* Penelope?" Edon asks.

"*The* Penelope," I mimic his tone.

Edon scratches behind his ear, reminding me of a canine movement. "Forgive me for being dumb. These photographs look current. Are you saying she's still alive?"

"That's exactly what we're saying," Violet answers. "Amelia ran into her six months ago."

Oliver raises his hand. "I hate to interrupt, but who is Penelope?"

Viktor slides forward in his seat. "Penelope was—is my wife."

"Why does she look just like Miss Lockhart?" He looks between the pictures and me. "Are you Penelope?"

I laugh. "No, been there, done that." Ollie looks

confused. "Harrison tried to turn me into her. It's a long story."

"We believe Amelia and Penelope are connected somehow, but no, Amelia is not Penelope." Viktor stands, moving across the room after he speaks. It's clear the conversation makes him uncomfortable, and I don't blame him.

"I'm still missing the connection of what this has to do with 'The Silver Bullets.'" Edon reads through the headlines of the clippings.

"You said you had reason to believe they were working with an ancient vampire. We believe Penelope is the ancient vampire you're talking about." Violet makes the connection for the two men.

"How ancient are we speaking?" Ollie asks.

"A thousand years old," Viktor answers.

"Shit."

"You took the words out of my mouth, Mr. Fitzgerald," Violet answers.

"You ran into her six months ago?" Edon asks me.

"I did. At the time, I didn't think it was relevant."

"How could running into an ancient vampire that was believed to have been dead for over two hundred years, not be relevant?" Edon asks.

"That's not important right now. What we need to focus on is why she's here and why she's working with the vigilantes," Viktor stops Edon's questions.

"The only way to find out is to send someone in." Edon stands, moving around the room. "We have to get someone on the inside. I have a few lycan I can ask."

"No," Viktor says. "They'll see right through a wolf. Subtlety is not your forte."

"I'll do it," I interrupt. All eyes in the room turn toward me.

"How do you think that's going to work?" Edon asks. "You look just like Penelope."

"I can dye my hair and wear contacts. I can do it."

"With all due respect, Miss Lockhart, you are a baby vampire, who barely understands the vampire ways. They'll see through you in a heartbeat." Oliver has a point.

"No, Amelia's right. Out of all of us, she's the most human. She's the only one who might be able to pull this off," Violet answers for the group. "I can take her to my hairdresser this afternoon." She moves to my side.

Viktor sighs. "I don't like it, but it just might work." He looks at me. "Do you really think you could do it?"

"Yes," I lie. Truth is, I have no clue if I can do it. I've never been a good actress. "Violet, make it happen."

She claps her hands together. "Let's go!" She pulls me toward the door and straight into her waiting SUV. She's on her phone and weaving in and out of traffic at the same time, driving us straight to her favorite salon. We complete the hour drive in forty minutes and find an entire crew of hairdressers waiting on us when we get there.

"Good afternoon, Miss Du Four. We have a team set

up for the afternoon." They usher me into the awaiting chair and begin discussing what they're going to do. I give Violet full design reign, and she's in her element.

While several stylists work on my coloring my hair, Violet keeps coming back into the salon, bringing bags of clothes and shoes on each trip. I'm facing away from the mirror but can tell the color of my hair has changed from my natural bright red coloring to dark brown. When I was younger, I was convinced people stared at me because of my hair, and they did. I hated it because of that reason. Now, seeing the red replaced makes me sad.

The stylist next to me pulls out a pair of shears, making a cut across the side of my face, cutting my hair even with my shoulders. I close my eyes as the rest of my hair is cut to the same length. I secretly wipe a tear, trying to hide the feelings that are attached to my hair.

Two hours, three rinses, two haircuts, a pair of brown contacts, and coloring later, my chair is turned toward the mirror. The woman staring back at me isn't me.

"Oh, my God! It's perfect!" Violet exclaims from behind. My hair has lost its natural curl, and my eyes are the same mousy brown color as my hair.

The team of stylists stands behind me, waiting on pins and needles for my response. "Thank you, ladies and gentlemen. I love it," I fake enthusiasm. The team claps for themselves, and I try to smile without giving away my true feelings.

Violet and I grab all of the shopping bags and head toward her SUV. It's not until I'm inside that I release the emotions hiding inside. "Amelia?" Violet asks, sliding into the driver's side seat.

"I'm sorry, I feel stupid for crying." I sniff loudly. "I've never felt any less like myself than I do right now."

"That's the whole point. Hair will grow. Even vampires have to get haircuts. You're right, you don't look anything like yourself, and that's what we need. You can't infiltrate them looking like Penelope."

I sniff loudly. "I know."

She pulls the car over. "This is why you're the only one with the ability to do this. You're more human than any of us. If anyone can pull this off, it's you."

I nod. She's right. I'm an emotional basket case. I'll fit right in. We don't say anything else as we drive across the lake and back to the house where I've lived for the past year. I help Violet carry in the piles of bags, setting them down to open the door. Celeste is waiting on the other side. The look on her face matches my inner turmoil perfectly.

"Amelia?"

"It's me," I answer.

"What happened?"

"I'm going to be leaving for a little while, but I promise I'll be back. I had to change the way I look to trick some people." I lower myself to her level.

"Will you come back?" Her voice sounds weak and small.

"Pinky promise." I hold my pinky toward her, and she wraps hers around mine.

"I don't like your hair or eyes like that."

"Yeah, I'm not a fan either."

"I have to go hide. The other vampire is here, and Daddy doesn't want him to see me." I nod, watching her climb the main stairs in silence.

off to college

VIOLET HELPS ME PACK, showing me each outfit before placing them into a suitcase. Our conversation has stayed light and away from the fact that I'm going to be pretending to be a vigilante for the Lord, or whatever their mantra is. A soft knock on the door draws me back to reality. "Come in."

Viktor opens the door and stares at me, making me even more self-conscious. "Wow," he says, staring at my hair. "If I didn't know better, I'd swear you were a stranger in my house."

Violet smiles, taking responsibility for my makeover. "I think she looks perfect."

"She doesn't look anything like Amelia, that's for sure." He clears his throat. "When you're ready, we've come up with a plan we think might work. Can you come downstairs?" I nod, regretting volunteering for this.

Violet and I enter the sitting room to find the three men waiting for us. Edon and Oliver stand as we enter. Both stare at me blankly. "Wow," Ollie says. "You have one hell of a stylist, Violet."

"Amelia, you look different," Edon says, raking me up and down with his eyes. I can't tell from his tone if he approves or disapproves.

I sit down and take a deep breath. "How am I supposed to find these people?"

"You don't. You let them find you," Ollie answers. "The attack on the lycan bar is the first in the city. But they're getting braver. It'll only be a matter of time until they attack again."

"True, but Drew went looking for them and brought them there. I need to be one of them."

"I've researched the young girl that killed herself," Viktor stands from his chair.

"Meredith," I remind them of her name.

"Yes, Meredith. She was barely eighteen years old and fresh out of high school. Her parents thought she was away at college. They had no idea she was a part of anything other than her classes. It seems she hadn't been to school in over a month and was living with the vigilantes somewhere in the city."

My mind flashes to me drinking her blood. I drank the blood of someone's daughter. She had her entire life ahead of her, and I drained her. "Excuse me," I say, running out of the room and up the stairs. A few minutes later there's a soft knock on my door.

"Amelia?" Viktor says, cracking the door. "May I come in?"

I wipe the tears streaming down my face. "Yes," I sob.

He sits on the edge of the bed, not far from where I'm sitting. "I didn't think about how hearing that would affect you." I sit up, wiping tears.

"She was just a kid lost in this world. Instead of helping her, I drank her blood." I pull my legs close to my chest, wrapping my arms around them. "I drained her blood, Viktor."

He slides close enough that his elbow touches my leg. "Amelia, you didn't kill her. She chose to take her own life, and there wasn't anything you could've said or done to change that. That's why what you're doing is so important. You couldn't save Meredith, but you can save the next Meredith." He pulls my chin up. "Look at me, mon amour." His eyes are softer as he keeps his hand under my chin. "It wasn't your fault."

"I know," I answer between sobs.

"No. It wasn't your fault," he repeats. "None of this is your fault." I lower my legs and fall into him, burying my head into his chest. The tears that flow are not just for Meredith. They're for this entire shit show I've been thrown into for the last year. To his credit, Viktor lets me cry it out.

"I sent the others home," he says after my tears have slowed enough that I'm able to breathe. "We'll discuss the plan when you're up to it." I pull away from the man who spent his spare time terrifying me after we met. If anyone had told me that a year later I'd be using him as a life-size tissue, I would never have believed it.

"Thank you." I wipe the tears from my face.

Viktor pulls away, straightening his waistcoat. "You're welcome. When you feel like it, come downstairs, and we'll figure everything out." He stands, moving toward the door, and turns back in my direction. "I like the new hair." He leaves me alone in my room.

Did Viktor just comfort and compliment me? I laugh at the irony and shove a few familiar sweatshirts into the suitcases. "Suck it up, Amelia. You have a job to do, and you're going to do it the best you can."

I head downstairs to find Viktor and Celeste playing a game in the sitting room. "Amelia!" Celeste says, moving toward me. "Want to play? Daddy's cheating."

"I am not cheating," Viktor says with a laugh. "Just admit you're not as good at poker as you think you are."

"You're playing poker?"

"Sure. Daddy says I'm a natural."

"I believe the words I just said are 'you're not as good as you think you are.'" He laughs at his daughter.

"Yeah, that's not what I heard," she answers.

"I don't think I want to play, but thank you for the invitation." I sit on the couch behind Celeste.

"It's fine. I'm getting bored with it anyway." Celeste gathers up the cards along with the stack of money in the middle of the table. "Later," she says, heading upstairs.

"She's a card shark." He laughs.

"I'm ready to figure this whole thing out," I announce.

Viktor slides back in his seat. "You're going back to college."

I laugh loudly. "I finally received my Ph.D. this year. I've spent my entire life in a school of some sort, and you want me to go back?"

"Yes."

He hands me a stack of papers. "You're registered under the name of Riley Smith, and you're majoring in general studies."

"General studies? What the hell? That means I'll be in the basic courses with people who don't know what they want to do with their lives."

"You'll fit right in." Ouch. It seems the Viktor who let me cry on his shoulder earlier is gone, replaced with the version I'm more familiar with. "Your first class starts at nine o'clock tomorrow morning." He pulls a schedule out of his pocket. "I took the opportunity to register you for the least number of hours, and you're moving into the dorm this evening."

"The dorm? Are you serious?"

He smiles. "Very. That's the best way to be recruited."

"How long do you think this will take?"

"Meredith only lived in the dorm for two weeks before she was indoctrinated and moved in with them."

"Viktor, I'm twenty-six years old. I'm not going to pass for a freshman."

"With that haircut, you could pass as a middle school student. Violet dropped off the items you'll need for your room already."

"Two weeks?"

"Or less if you play your cards right. I'm going to get your bags." He returns, carrying my bags, moments later. "I'll drive you."

We pull in front of Tulane University an hour later. The redbrick building we park in front of looks original to the campus. "Is this the dorm I'm moving into?"

"It's where all freshmen live."

"It looks haunted," I answer.

"Probably is." He parks illegally in the fire lane and pops the trunk.

"I don't think you're supposed to park here."

Viktor looks at the signs and shrugs. "Oh, well."

It doesn't take long to unload and take my items to the second floor. Luckily the room is for a single occupant, and I'm grateful I won't have to share a room with an actual teenager. "God, this brings back memories."

"Good or bad?" he asks.

"Neither. Just memories." He stays, helping me unpack my room and make up the bed like a typical freshman would. He also fills the refrigerator with packets of blood, disguised as soft drinks. A loud knock on the door interrupts my unpacking. I open the door to find a young girl with bright pink hair leaning against the doorframe.

"Hi! I'm your RA, Samantha. Welcome to Tulane."

I smile. "Thank you." I hold my hand out to her. "Am..." Viktor coughs loudly, interrupting me.

"*Riley*, don't you want to check your schedule?" he asks.

"Oh, yes. I'll do that in a minute. Riley Smith," I say, shaking the RA's hand. I can't help but notice Samantha sizing up Viktor. She flips her pink ponytail, trying to grab his attention.

"I'll be going," he says before handing me a new cell phone on his way out of the door. "This is in case you need me. It's a direct line to my phone." He wraps his arm around my neck, pulls me close, and kisses me on the forehead. "Goodbye, sweetheart. I'll see you soon."

Samantha stares at his backside the entire way down the hall. As soon as he's out of earshot, she asks the question I knew was coming. "Is that your dad?" I swear I hear him chuckle.

I cough before answering. "No, not quite. Viktor's my uncle. I've lived with him for the past year."

"Damn, your uncle is hot. Is he single?"

"Nope. He's very married and has a kid. He's way older than he looks. Good night." I close the door on my visitor, annoyed that she thinks Viktor is hot. My new phone vibrates from a text.

Uncle? Really?

Yes, the creepy kind.

He sends a frowny face emoji. I can't hide the smile his text brings. Teasing Viktor has become one of my favorite pastimes.

With the dorm asleep, I take the opportunity to sneak through each floor and open rooms, looking for anything that might give me a clue of how to throw myself at the group of vigilantes. In the downstairs common room, I'm surprised to see a young man sitting alone in the back corner. I turn, heading the other way, hoping he doesn't see me when he calls out. "Can't sleep either?"

I stop, turning toward him. "No, I guess not."

"Feel free to join me. I'm watching a stimulating television show about sperm whales."

"That does sound appealing." I sit a few chairs away from the young man. He looks around eighteen and fresh out of high school. "Riley," I say, turning toward him.

"Josh," he answers with a small wave. "Nice to meet you, Riley."

"So, what are we learning about sperm whales?"

He shrugs. "I don't know. It's just on. Honestly, I'm sitting here contemplating life, and whether it's worth it in the long run."

His words draw my attention away from the whales. "What do you mean?"

"I don't know. Just rambling."

"What are you majoring in, Josh?"

"Biochemical engineering. You?"

"General studies for now. I'm leaning toward history of some sort."

"Yawn," he answers.

"I could say the same for biochemical engineering." Josh stares at the screen, and I can tell his eyelids are getting heavier. "Why don't you go to bed? You look tired."

"My roommate's a vampire," he answers. "I don't want to be dinner."

"A vampire?"

He turns toward me. "I know how crazy I sound, but I swear he's a vampire."

"Has he tried to drink from you?"

He shakes his head. "No."

"Has he ever threatened you?"

"No."

"Then why do you think he's a vampire?"

Josh shrugs. "He never sleeps, has blood in the refrigerator, and watches me like a cat stalking its prey." His head falls again, almost asleep.

"Get some sleep. I'll stay here and protect you from the vampire." I almost laugh at the irony.

"You'd do that? Thanks." He doesn't waste a minute

before his eyes close and he's sound asleep. I pull my new phone out and send a text to Viktor.

> Made a friend. He thinks his roommate is a vampire.

> LOL!

> Do you even know what that means?

He sends the middle finger emoji along with a Snapchat. I open the chat to see a video of Celeste. She's sitting at the table, and it looks like they're playing a game of some sort. "Be careful, Amelia!" she says through the video. The camera moves to Viktor's face.

"Yes, be careful, and yes, I know what LOL means." He rolls his eyes and shows me his middle finger before the video shuts off. I make a quick reply video, telling Celeste goodnight and return the finger for Viktor. I look over at my new friend who's sound asleep in an uncomfortable chair. It's going to be a long two weeks.

SIX

first meeting

THE SUN BEGINS to rise before Josh moves. I'd almost be convinced he died during his sleep if it weren't for his heavy breathing. I watched four nature documentaries, surfed the entire internet, and wandered around the room thirty times while he slept.

"You stayed," he says, stretching his arms and legs in front of him.

"I promised I would." I smile. "But I need to get ready for my first class and grab something to eat."

"Sure, thanks again." I wave, leaving my new friend in his makeshift bed for the night. Back in my room, I open one of the "Cokes" and drink it in one gulp. Thankfully my room has a private bathroom, and I enjoy a hot shower. I don't know what Viktor had to do to secure that for me, but I'm grateful. Packing my backpack with freshman essentials, I head out of the dorm and across campus to the History building.

I find the classroom without much trouble and choose a seat in the back of the classroom. History 101 with a room full of freshmen is the definition of torture. Thankfully, the class passes quickly and painlessly. I'm almost the last person out of the room when the professor calls me back. "Riley?" It takes me a minute to remember that's me. I'm Riley.

"Yes, sir?" I turn back, standing in front of the desk.

"I was watching you during class. You seemed more interested than most. If you ever need help with any of your classes, I'd be happy to help you." He smiles a creepy grin. He looks to be in his mid-forties with salt-and-pepper gray hair.

"Thank you, I'll keep that in mind." He touches my shoulder as I turn to leave. I pull my phone out of my pocket, feeling it vibrate.

> How was your first class?

> It sucked. My professor is creepy.

> Creepy how?

> As in mid-life crises. He hit on me, I think.

> Let me know if your hot uncle needs to pay him a visit.

I can think of nothing more embarrassing than that. I'm good.

I exit the building, pulling my schedule out of my pocket. My next class isn't until two o'clock. What am I going to do until then? I wander into the library, searching the bulletin boards for anything exciting, and find nothing. I make my way to the school computers and begin searching for information on missing students. Other than Meredith, eight students have disappeared without contacting their parents over the past year. Police reports were filed, but there's been no contact with any of them. I write the names down, not sure if they're related, but it's a start. I search each name, unable to find any information on any of them. I give up and head to the mythological creatures section. Searching for books on vampires, I pull a few that I haven't seen before from the shelves.

"You like vampires?" a voice asks beside me.

I turn, seeing a young girl with dark hair and eyes. "I guess. I've never thought much about them, real ones I mean. I love reading books about them."

She smiles. "Yes. Team Edward all the way." I laugh, trying not to look offended at her version of vampires.

"What about wolves?" I ask.

"Do you think they really exist?"

I shrug. "If we believe in vampires, then we have to believe in wolves."

She smiles, holding her hand toward me. "Zoe."

"Riley," I answer, shaking her hand. "It's good to meet a fellow believer."

"Want to go grab a coffee?"

"Sure. Let me get my stuff. My next class isn't until two." She follows me to my backpack, and we walk across campus to the coffee shop.

"What would you like? My treat."

"I'm not a huge coffee drinker. You choose."

Zoe smiles widely. "I like that idea." She orders something that I made a hundred times in my former life as a barista while I find a table in the corner.

> Getting coffee with a vampire/werewolf fan.

> What?

Viktor answers.

> I'll tell you later...

My phone buzzes several times, and I ignore it as Zoe brings the two huge cups of coffee to the table. "This looks amazing," I lie. It looks gross, and I dread having to pretend to drink it.

"Tell me about yourself, Riley." Zoe sits across from me.

"There's really not much to tell. I graduated last summer and transferred here after my parents kicked me out. I don't have any family, so I'm here to gain a new one."

"Your story sounds familiar," Zoe says, taking a drink from her coffee. "My parents are both dead."

"Oh, I'm sorry."

"I'm not," she answers. "They were dumb." I don't know what to say to that.

"So, team Edward or Jacob?" she asks.

"Oh, Edward, all the way." This is the most immature conversation I've had in a long time. "I mean, Jacob is hot and all, but I like Edward's angsty ways."

"What if I told you they were real?"

"Edward and Jacob?" I ask, playing dumb.

Zoe laughs. "No, vampires and werewolves. And they're nothing like the books."

"You mean vampires don't sparkle?"

"Or drink anything besides human blood. They're killers." She smiles. "You probably think I'm crazy now, don't you?"

"Is it crazy if I say no? I saw something once when I was a kid. I've always thought they were real."

Zoe pulls a piece of paper from her backpack, handing it to me. "If you really believe, you should join us."

"V.O.W.? What does that mean?"

"Vamps or wolves, silly. We meet three times a week at an abandoned church in the Quarter. Think about it, and let me know if you'd like to come." She scribbles her name and phone number on the top of the paper before leaving me alone at the table.

What the hell was that? Could this be the vigilante group or some psychotic teenagers who desperately want to be the stars of a paranormal romance book?

> I think I found something about the group.

> You've been there not even twelve hours.

> I know, but I was invited to a weird meeting.

I send a picture of the flyer to him.

> Looks like groupies.

> Could be, or could be vigilantes.

He sends a rolling-eye emoji. For someone who couldn't even figure out how to slide the phone screen a year ago, he's picked up texting and emojis pretty fast.

> Keep looking. Celeste says to make sure you drink the blood.

It's my turn to send the rolling-eye emoji.

> Yes, Mom.

I send a heart afterward and instantly regret it. What if Viktor thinks the heart is for him? A few minutes pass before I receive a response.

I knew you were obsessed with me.

I put my phone in my pocket without responding. I trek my way across campus, and for the first time since transforming into a vampire, I notice the students "notice" me. Not everyone responds, but several do, and it surprises me. A young girl stops walking toward me and turns, taking a wide path around me. A group of boys, standing by the fountain in the square, stop talking as I approach and stare at me like predators. What the hell? Their behavior reminds me of how the group of women reacted to Harrison in the Quarter. Their eyes follow me until I'm safely inside the English Language Arts building.

I shake off the weirdness and make my way into the large theater on the bottom floor. Since every freshman is required to take this course, I'm here with at least one hundred of my closest friends. I find a seat toward the bottom and pull out the laptop Viktor bought for the facade.

"Welcome, ladies and gentlemen. My name is Dr. Oliver Fitzgerald, and I will be filling in for your professor for the next few weeks." I close my laptop and stare at the vampire in front of me. Whispers and giggles surround me as the students take a moment to look at our new teacher. He's wearing skin-tight black jeans, a black V-neck T-shirt, and a deep gray sport coat. He knew what he was doing when he dressed this morning. Between the accent and the looks, half of the people in the room just fell in love. He winks in my direction, and I spontaneously roll my eyes.

I pull my phone out, snap a picture of Professor Ollie, and send it to Viktor. He sends back a laughing emoji, tempting me to throw my phone to the front of the room. Although I'd never admit it, Ollie does a decent job teaching the class. Afterward, there's a line of groupies ready to ask him questions. "Excuse me, ladies and gentlemen." He steps away from the line and heads straight toward me.

"Miss Smith." He nods.

"*Dr.* Fitzgerald." I roll my eyes, packing everything into my backpack. "When did you become an English Professor?"

"You learn quite a few things when you live for as long as we do. May I escort you to your next class?"

"My next class is tomorrow." I pull out the schedule Viktor left for me. "It seems I'm not registered for much."

"Aye, we tried to keep your schedule light."

"We...did you have your hand in this whole thing?"

He smiles without answering. We continue walking until no one else is in sight. "Have you found anything that could be useful?" I pull the V.O.W. flyer from my pocket, handing it to him. "What is this?"

"A girl named Zoe gave it to me this afternoon. I was looking through the vampire books in the library, and she started talking to me. I don't know if it's anything important, but it didn't take long to get it."

"You think it's related?" he asks.

I shrug. "I have no clue. She told me if I was interested in going, to call her."

"Did you call her?"

I snatch the paper away from him. "I literally got this a few hours ago. I wanted to see what Viktor thought, first. I sent him a picture."

"What was the verdict?"

"He thinks it's just paranormal groupies." I fold the paper, sliding it back in my pocket.

"He could be right, but it's worth looking into. Wait a day or so, and give her a call. It won't hurt to check into it." He turns toward the parking lot. "In the meantime, make sure you complete your homework, and I expect a three-page essay on the history of vampires by our next class."

I unzip my backpack and hand him a hardbound copy of my doctoral thesis on the *History of Mythological Creatures in Europe*.

"What's this?"

"My essay." I turn, walk away, and leave him holding a copy of what got me into this mess to start with.

SEVEN

vlad, the college freshman

NOT SURPRISINGLY, I find Josh, curled up in an extremely small chair, staring at a nature documentary on the snowy television. "You're back," he mumbles as I enter the common room.

"I am. Still not sleeping in your room?"

"No. I don't feel like getting eaten."

I laugh. "Is your roommate in your room?"

"Why else would I be here?"

I move closer to my snarky friend. "Let's go meet him."

Josh looks at me. "Are you one of them?"

"One of who?"

"You know. Those crazed vampire girls that come to college in New Orleans, hoping to meet their Edward."

"No, I'm more into wolves." I nudge his shoulder. "Introduce me to him. I kind of have a sixth sense about these things."

He sighs. "You promise you won't throw yourself at him?"

I hold up my hand, flashing three fingers. "Scouts honor."

"Alright." He moans standing from the chair and leads me down the hallway to the last room on the first floor. "You ready for this?"

"Let's do it." He opens the door to a pitch-black room.

"Vlad? Are you awake?" I can barely contain the laughter begging to escape. Vlad? Not very original. A loud hiss sounds from the back corner of the room.

"Joshua, why didst thou let the light in?" Oh, my God. Josh turns on the overhead light, and a boy with dark brown hair scurries to the corner of his bed. He's wearing a cape and quickly sweeps it around his face, covering his eyes. "The light is burning me."

"Vlad, this is Riley. She's never seen a vampire before." I look at my new friend. If only he could appreciate the irony of this conversation.

"Hi, Vlad." I wave. "Do you need anything?"

"Darkness..." he whispers.

"Ok. Josh, I think we better leave him alone for now." Josh nods, following me out of the room. We walk in silence back to the common room.

"See what I mean?" he asks, once in the safety of the outdated room.

"I see, but I'm here to tell you, he's not a vampire."

"How can you be sure?"

"You're going to have to trust me on this. I've lived in New Orleans my entire life and have run into a few vampires over the years. Your roommate isn't one of them."

Josh takes a deep breath. "That's good to know. I'm still not sleeping in there." Honestly, I don't blame him. "Vlad" may not be a vampire, but he's a few sandwiches short of a picnic. He might bite his neck in the middle of the night out of delusion.

"Here." I hand him my dorm key. "I can't sleep. You can take my room."

"I can't take your room."

"Sure, you can. I'll come back tomorrow morning. You look like you could use some rest."

He rubs the key with his fingers. "Thank you, Riley. I don't know what to say." I watch him sneak upstairs to the girl's floor. I wait until he disappears before pulling my phone out.

> Met the vampire roommate.

> And?

> He spoke in old English and was wearing a cape.

> I'm speechless.

> Haha. That's a first. There's nothing to do at night. I'm bored.

He doesn't answer, and I decide to wander around campus. I make my way toward the football stadium. I've never been to a college football game in all the years I've been enrolled in college. Staring through the gates, the field looks larger than it does on television.

"Thinking of becoming a cheerleader?" I turn toward the source of a very familiar voice. Viktor's leaning against a large oak tree on the other side of the gate. He's wearing skinny jeans and a fitted sweater.

"No. More along the lines of a quarterback. I'm fast, especially now," I answer with a smile. "You didn't text me back."

"You mentioned you were bored. I thought my company may remedy that situation."

"Look at you, thinking about someone besides yourself." My voice is laced with sarcasm.

"Let's go for a walk." He pulls a key to the gate from his pocket, unlocks it, and walks through.

"Do I want to know why you have a key to the football stadium at Tulane University?"

"Probably not." I wrap my arm through his, and he leads me to the front of the stadium. "Would you like a tour?"

"Sure?" He unlocks the glass doors that lead into the training center and gift shop and stops in front of a large plaque.

"Luquire Memorial Stadium?" I turn to look at the vampire. "Is this named after you?"

"Technically, yes. Figuratively, no. It's amazing what a few million dollars will buy you."

"I'm guessing so." We tour the locker rooms, gift shop, and exercise room where Viktor points out each item and its benefits for the team. The more he talks, the more I'm surprised.

"How do you know all this?"

He shrugs. "It's my job. I designed this building and its contents, donated a few million dollars, and bam... it's named after my company." I stop walking, staring at the stranger I thought I knew. "What?"

"You have a job?"

Viktor laughs. "Did you think I laid around the house all day, playing board games with Celeste?"

"Maybe?"

"I assure you, Amelia. I'm not all brawn and good looks. There are some brains behind these eyes."

"Your eyes are a different color tonight."

He smiles. "What color are they?"

"Brown, because you're full of shit." I playfully punch his shoulder. "I believe you about the job, but you lost me at brawn and good looks."

"Tell me about the flyer you received," he changes the subject. I pull it out of my pocket, unfolding it for him.

"You still think they're groupies?" I ask.

"Most likely, but getting in touch with this girl won't hurt. See if it leads you anywhere."

"Ollie suggested the same thing."

"You talked to Oliver about this?" He folds the paper, handing it back to me.

"I showed it to him after English class." He locks the doors behind us, leading me out of the building.

"Your tour will continue with the library," he says.

"I beat you to that one. That was where I met our friend with the flyer."

"I bet you didn't have the keys to the secured book section." He holds a set of keys in front of my face. He smiles, and we head across campus to the brick building, original to the university.

The smell hits me first. "I love the smell of old books."

"Smells like mildew and mold to me." He leads me to a room in the back corner of the library. "I donated many of these books over the years." He opens the door to a room with books that rival both his and Harrison's libraries. I can't help but run my fingers over the spines.

"This is great."

"Penelope collected most of the ones in my library. She loved books as much as you do." He stops walking. "I can't wrap my head around the fact that she may be alive and in New Orleans."

For the first time since I've known him, Viktor peeled off a layer of protective skin he keeps over himself. "Do you want to talk about it?"

He looks up, sadness covers his face. "I don't know." I wrap my arm through his and lead him toward a bench in the middle of the room.

"Sit. We're going to talk about it."

He rolls his eyes but follows directions. "I don't know what to say."

"How do you feel?"

He laughs awkwardly. "Why does this feel like an episode of Dr. Phil?"

"How do you feel?" I repeat.

He takes a deep breath. "Angry, sad, hurt, pissed off...shall I continue?"

"It's okay to feel all those things."

"This is really starting to feel like Dr. Phil." He smirks.

"You've spent a century building those walls of sarcasm you surround yourself with. Let them down for a bit." Viktor looks at the floor. "I'm sorry for what she did."

"It's not your fault, mon amour."

"No, it's not. But I'm sorry that you and Celeste have had to go through the pain of thinking she's dead." Viktor lays his hand on top of mine, and I swear a tear streams down his cheek.

"Thank you," he whispers. "If I find her, I don't know how I'll react."

"What do you mean?"

He takes a deep breath. "I don't know if I'll want to kill her or make love to her."

I laugh at his admission. "I'm not sure either of those is the best choice."

"I'm sorry for the way I treated you when we first met."

I look down, not wanting to remember that time in my life. "You already apologized."

"No, not really. I'm truly sorry, Amelia. I hope one day you'll be able to forgive me. I was a complete ass and for no other reason than you looked like Penelope." His hand is still on top of mine, and surprisingly, I'm not in a hurry for it to leave.

"Forgiven." I stand. "I have an idea." He raises his eyebrows. "Let's go scare the shit out of Vlad."

"The vampire kid?"

"The very same one. Josh deserves to be able to sleep in his room without the fear of being eaten, no matter how off base it is."

"I like how you think." Viktor locks up the secret room and follows me to the ancient dorms. The common room is empty, which means Josh is most likely still in my room. We move quietly to the door of the room he shares with Vlad.

"How are we doing this?" I ask.

"Leave it to me." Viktor scratches his fingernails on the wooden door and whispers the boy's name.

"Josh?" a scared voice sounds through the door. Viktor scratches the door a second time.

"Open the door, my child." Viktor's voice sounds different than normal.

"Who's there?" Vlad's accent has changed from Old English to scared shitless.

"Open the door, my child, and you shall see." The door creaks open, slowly.

"Hello? Who are you?"

Viktor smiles, showing his fangs. He nudges me with his elbow, and I do the same. "We've heard there's an unregistered vampire living here."

"That's simply not allowed," I add. "We're going to need you to come with us."

"Where?" Vlad's voice sounds extremely scared, and I almost feel guilty.

"To the Vampire Registration Society," Viktor answers.

"I...I'm not a real vampire. I just like pretending..." Vlad stutters over his words.

Viktor turns toward me. "Do you think the council will believe he's made this entire thing up?"

"I don't. I think the VRS will need to see a change in order to truly believe he's not a vampire."

"I will!" Vlad exclaims. He rips the cape off, throws it in a nearby trash can, and spits the fake teeth to the floor. "See, it's just pretend."

"We've also heard talks of threats to your roommate."

Vlad laughs awkwardly. "Josh is my best friend."

"What do you think, Number 2?"

I pretend to study Vlad from head to toe. "I think it might just work, Number 3." Viktor nods.

"Vlad, make sure you follow through. We will be watching."

"Roger. My name is Roger."

"We'll be watching, Roger," I say as the door closes.

"Okay," he whispers through the door. I can barely contain my laughter. Once outside, Viktor and I both erupt into spontaneous hysterics.

"Did you see that kid's face?" he asks.

I reach up, giving him a high five. "That was the most fun I've had in a while," I answer. We laugh for another ten minutes before reality strikes. "Do you think we traumatized him?"

"Probably, but from what you said, he needed it. I don't think he's going to be threatening to eat anyone ever again." Viktor's smile turns serious. "Thank you, Amelia."

"For what?"

"For allowing me to have fun. I haven't had fun in a very long time."

"That's me." I laugh. "For a good time, call!"

He doesn't return my laughter. "I'm serious. Thank you." He reaches over, takes my hand into his, and kisses the back of it. His lips linger longer than they should, and I don't pull away. I clear my throat, not sure what or if I should say anything.

"Maybe we can scare someone else tomorrow night."

"It's a plan," he answers. The sun is beginning to crest over the horizon, meaning students will be milling around campus before too much longer. I head back up the stairs of my dorm, this time going all the way to the second floor. What just happened? Did we turn a corner? Are we friends? I peek out the stairwell landing window to see the spot where Viktor stood is empty. I pull out my phone.

> Tell Celeste I miss her, and thanks again for coming.

He sends a heart emoji in return. I wait a few minutes, not sure how to respond. Finally, my snarkiness wins.

> I knew you were obsessed with me.

I copy his message from yesterday.

EIGHT

sugar daddies

I KNOCK LIGHTLY on my room door. "Josh?"

"Who is it?" he answers, using a high-pitched voice.

"It's me." The door cracks open, and he scours the hallway. "Did you sleep well?" I ask, squeezing through the crack.

"I slept amazingly. Thank you. It was much more comfortable than the chair."

"Good. I think you'll feel comfortable in your own room from now on. Roger decided he wasn't a vampire anymore."

He laughs. "I almost forgot his real name. Did you talk to him?"

"I did. He told me you two were best friends."

"We were, or I guess we are. He's been going through a rough patch lately. I was seriously beginning to question whether or not he really was a vampire."

"I can assure you he's not." Josh hands me the key to my room.

"Thanks again." He takes a last glance around my room. "Your family must have a lot of money. This room is nicer than most."

I shrug. "I guess. More like I have a rich benefactor."

"Like a sugar daddy?"

Picturing Viktor as a sugar daddy makes me laugh loudly. "Not quite. Just a friend who wants to see me succeed."

Josh straightens my bed before moving toward the door. "Thanks again. I'm going to head back to my room and see how Roger acts."

Sitting on the edge of the bed, I look around the small room. If this is nice, I'd hate to see the rest. Maybe Viktor should put some of his money into refurbishing the freshmen dorms. My first class this morning isn't until ten o'clock and is general science, followed by psychology at one. I gather my backpack and head toward the science building. Just like all freshmen general classes, the room is packed. I find a seat toward the top and pull out my laptop. "Hey!" Zoe, the girl from the library, slides into the seat next to me.

"Hi!" I fake enthusiasm.

"Be prepared for this class."

"Why?"

She nods her head toward the professor. "See the professor?" I stare at the middle-aged woman at the front of the room and nod. "She's a wolf," she continues.

"What?"

"You heard me. She's a wolf. They're not all huge, muscular, and gorgeous like they are in books and movies."

"Yeah, but she looks like a grandmother." Zoe shrugs at my words. "What makes you so sure?"

"See the pointed hairline in front?" I nod, waiting for more information. She doesn't say anything else.

"That's it? That's the reason you think she's a lycanthrope?"

"That and she hangs out at a few of the bars in the Quarter." I look up at her words.

"What kind of bars?" I ask.

"You know, the kind where the wolves hang out." Maybe this girl knows more than she's letting on. I decide to play dumb.

"Do you really think they hang out together in the Quarter?" Zoe turns completely toward me.

"I don't think, I know. You should come to one of our meetings." She hands me another V.O.W. flyer.

"I think maybe I will." Zoe's eyes light up.

"That's great! There's a meeting tonight. You should come." She tugs a piece of paper out of a spiral-bound notebook and scribbles an address on it. "It starts at seven." I stare at the numbers written on the page. I'm still not sure if this is the vigilante group or just a group of kids with some sort of book club, but there's only one way to find out.

Luckily, the professor doesn't keep the class the entire hour, and I'm able to get back to my room quickly. I don't hesitate to send Viktor a text.

> I'm invited to a meeting of the V.O.W. tonight in the Quarter.

He responds within seconds.

> That's great. What time do I need to pick you up?

> I don't remember inviting you.

> It's assumed.

I send a rolling eyes emoji.

> I'll be at your dorm at five.

> Josh thinks I have a sugar daddy.

He responds with a GIF of a bag of sugar wearing a mustache, and I resend the rolling eyes.

Luckily, my psychology class is in the building next to the dorms, which makes for a quick commute. This class only has around thirty students, making it my smallest one yet. "Riley!" a voice calls across the court-yard. I hear the words, but it doesn't register that someone is speaking to me until I hear my real name. "Amelia," the voice whisper-yells. I turn, finding Ollie.

"Sorry, I keep forgetting my undercover name."

"Have you found any more information?"

I hand him the paper with the address on it. "I'm going to a meeting tonight. Viktor is picking me up at five."

He takes a picture of the address with his phone. "I'll do some research on the location."

"Thanks. Do you know any of the other professors?"

"A few, why?"

I shake the paper at him. "The girl that gave this to me is convinced the science teacher is a wolf."

"Dr. Moon?"

"Yeah, how'd you know?"

Ollie laughs. "Zoe's right. She is a wolf." I stare at the vampire in front of me. How many people have I known or come in contact with through the years that were lycan or vampire, and I had no clue? "I'll let you or Viktor know what I find out about the address." He turns, and like the rest of the girls on campus, I stare at his ass until he's out of sight.

I spend the next few hours in the library, searching old articles on any deaths that were unordinary or unusual. In New Orleans, that's a lot to go through. I'm beginning to feel like my eyes are crossing when a picture pops onto the computer screen. It's an old black-and-white photo and looks to be from around the early nineteen hundreds. A young girl with dark hair and eyes is standing in front of a dilapidated New Orleans mansion. Her dress is torn and dirty, and her tights have an entire knee missing. I stare into the young girl's eyes. Something about them is so familiar, so haunting. Underneath her image are written three letters, O.M.C. circa 1905. I take a screenshot of the photograph and send it to the nearest printer. I glance at my phone and realize I have a missed text from Viktor, and it's getting close to five.

On my way.

I head straight to the dorm and stare into the closet. What does one wear to a vigilante meeting? I decide on a pair of jeans, combat boots, and a denim jacket. Violet could be a personal shopper for the rich and famous. Every piece of clothing fits like it was made for me. True to his word, there's a soft knock on my door at five o'clock on the dot. I open the door to see Samantha, the residence assistant, with Viktor, standing behind her.

"Your uncle wanted to come up to see you, so I thought I'd escort him since technically, this is a girls-only floor."

He flashes a wicked smile. "Thank you, mon amour." His accent is more pronounced as he turns on the charm, kissing the back of her hand, and making her giggle.

"Any time." She stands at the door without moving.

"I'll take it from here," I say, closing the door in her face.

Viktor chuckles. "Such a sweet young lady."

"That sweet young lady wants in your pants."

He sits on my bed, propping his feet on the desk chair. "She'll have to stand in line."

I laugh out loud. "Will she be patron number one?"

He covers his heart with his hands. "You wound me." He looks me up and down. "You look like a badass this evening."

"In case you missed it, I *am* badass."

He stands. "You're right. I missed it. Ready to go?"

I follow him down the hall to the stairs, where Samantha is leaning against the doorframe. An extra button is open on her shirt, revealing the top of her breasts and the crease between. "Have a good evening, Mr. Luquire."

"Good evening to you, Samantha," he responds. She stays in place as we head down the stairs, smiling as we pass.

"Did you ever get that STD to clear up?" I ask loud enough that she can hear from upstairs.

Viktor's deep laugh echoes off the walls as we exit into the common room. "If I didn't know better, I'd think you were jealous." I join his laughter before climbing into the SUV. Am I jealous? Nah, I don't think of Viktor like that. He's more like the annoying uncle that gets on everyone's nerves. "Where are we going?" I hand him the paper with the address written on it.

"The meeting's not until seven. We have a few hours to kill." I pull the screenshot I took in the library out of my bag. "Do you recognize this house?"

He studies the picture for a while. "It looks familiar, but I can't place it." I take the picture back, looking into the eyes of the young girl. "What are you thinking?"

"I don't know. I was searching through old records of New Orleans for anything that might help us and ran across this. Something about the little girl feels familiar to me."

He takes the picture back. "These pillars." He points to four large pillars across the front of the porch. "They look like some of the houses that were on the river and in the bayou. Most of them have been destroyed, but some are still standing. We don't have time before your meeting, but we can check them out another day."

"I'd like that."

"Oh, I almost forgot." He hands me a folded piece of construction paper with neatly cutout hearts covering the front. "Celeste sent this." Nestled in the middle of the hearts she's written "Amelia" in perfect cursive. On the inside is a hand-drawn picture of the two of us, flying a kite. Her artwork is worthy of a museum.

"This is beautiful." I wipe a tear. "Did she do the artwork?"

He glances at the card. "She did. She's always had an eye for art."

"An eye? This is spectacular." I run my fingers over

the image of the small girl hanging in the air. "I miss her."

"She misses you, too. She's worried something's going to happen to you."

I laugh. "She thinks she's my mother." Viktor pulls the car away from the curb.

"That, she does. We have a few hours to kill before the meeting. I thought maybe you'd like to go for a walk by the river first."

"Sure." I shrug. "I'm always up for outdoor activities." He's driving at least ten miles under the speed limit. "You know, for a thousand-year-old vampire, you drive like an old man."

He laughs loudly. "Technically, I am an old man. Better to be safe than sorry. Have you seen the way some of these humans drive?" We pull up to Audubon Park, along with half of New Orleans. "Seems a lot of people had the same idea. We can go somewhere else if you like."

"No, I'm good." We move closer to the water, away from the crowds. "I always like coming here. It's a hidden oasis in the middle of a bustling city." We walk underneath an ancient live oak tree, sitting on the exposed roots, and I take a deep breath. "Not that I don't love coming to this park, but I get the feeling you brought me here for other reasons."

"That obvious, huh?" Viktor looks across the water, crossing his legs at the ankle. "I haven't been completely honest with you about Penelope." I turn, waiting for him to finish. "I had an idea she might still be alive."

"What?"

"After I found Celeste, I heard rumors that she was still around and living with Chamberlin."

I stand, turning toward the vampire I thought had become my friend. "You knew she was alive?"

"No. I heard rumors but never had any definitive answers."

"Why the hell not?"

"Celeste had barely gotten over the fact of her mother dying. Suddenly finding out she was alive didn't seem like a priority."

I cross my arms over my chest. "If her mother is still alive, she deserves to know the truth."

Viktor stands, matching my energy. "If her mother is still alive and abandoned her, knowing that would be worse."

He's right. Losing a parent because they died is different than losing a parent because they didn't want you anymore. "Celeste isn't an ordinary kid. She could handle it."

"You're probably right, but I didn't want her to be put in that situation."

"So, you let her live with Harrison and never looked?"

He kicks a tree root. "I didn't want to know the truth. If she was still alive, she didn't just abandon

Celeste, she abandoned me, too. I realize now how selfish I sound."

I didn't think about it like that. For the first time since meeting Viktor, he seems human and vulnerable. "No, you don't sound selfish. You sound broken."

"When you found those pictures, it confirmed the rumors."

"Harrison thought she was dead, too. Seems like she fooled both of you."

He laughs awkwardly. "She was kind of a bitch that way."

"Do you think the group of vigilantes is working with her?"

He moves closer to the edge of the river. "Hell, I don't know. Knowing her, probably."

I step to his side. "I'm sorry."

"Don't be, mon amour. It's not your fault." I wrap my arm around his elbow.

"No, but it hurt you, and I'm sorry you had to go through that." Viktor places his hand on top of mine, letting it linger as we continue walking.

"You're not what I expected when we first met," he admits.

"What did you expect?"

"I'm not sure, but I'm glad I was wrong."

NINE

i didn't sign up for this

WE PULL past the abandoned building at exactly seven o'clock, parking a few blocks away. "Are you sure this is it?" I hold the address up, looking at the dilapidated remains.

"Yes. This building has been home to many things over the years. Most recently, a church. Before that, a funeral home, and before that a brothel. It's perfect for a group of vigilantes. Oliver texted me the information he found in the city archives." He hands me a small earpiece. "Put this in your ear so I can hear what's going on. If you have any problems, don't hesitate to call me."

"You're not going inside?"

"No, I think it's better if you go alone. You were the one invited, and they'll be expecting you alone." I slide the small earpiece inside my ear, covering it with my hair.

87

"We need a code word." He looks at me like I've lost my mind. "You know, a word that when you hear me say it, you know I'm in trouble."

"That's actually a great idea. Hamburger."

"What?"

"That's your code word."

I stare at the vampire in front of me. "Why hamburger?"

"It was the first thing that came to mind. Just go with it."

I take a deep breath before leaving the safety of the SUV and head toward the address. Coming to the front door that's barely hanging on by two of the three hinges, I don't know if I should knock or just go in. I decide to knock. Nothing happens. I try again, this time hitting it hard enough the entire door shakes. Just like before, nothing happens. I send a quick text to Viktor.

> Are you sure this is the right place? No one answered the door.

> Just go in.

He follows up his text with a hamburger emoji. Someone needs to delete the emoji option from his phone.

I do as he suggests and turn the knob on the door. Surprisingly, it's unlocked. The inside looks as run down as the outside. The room I enter is dark and dingy, and the concrete floors are covered in holes and dark stains. Other than the occasional squeak from a mouse, the room is empty. "Hello?" I call, not really sure I want an answer.

Something similar to chanting comes from a room behind this one. Did I imagine that? "Hello?" I call again. I follow the sounds, leaving the empty room and moving into a hallway. I don't know why I'm scared. I'm a vampire. They should be the ones who are scared. The further I move, the louder the chanting becomes.

"Kill them all," echoes to my ears. I stop moving.

"Viktor, if you can hear me, this sucks. They're chanting." My phone buzzes.

> I can hear them. If you don't feel safe, leave.

"I'm good," I whisper. A door at the end of the hallway opens, revealing a familiar face.

"Riley?" Zoe stands in the doorframe. She's dressed in all black and wearing a black bandana around her neck. "I didn't think you'd actually come."

"You invited me," I answer.

She smiles. "Come on back. Everyone is back here." She opens the door wide, motioning me toward it. Walking through the door, I'm shocked by what I see. The room still looks like a sanctuary, however, there are no holy relics of any kind, only a poster-sized photograph of a man I remember from their website. Their leader, Gregory Stephens, sits beside his image. He's a large man with his stomach hanging over the waistband of the pants. Sitting there, he reminds me of Jabba the Hutt.

"Who is this, Zoe?" the man asks. His voice is soft and lacks emotion.

"This is Riley. She's a friend from school."

"Welcome, Riley," the group chants in unison. This feels like a bad movie.

"Welcome, my child," Gregory says. "My name is Greg, and you are loved."

"You are loved," the group echoes.

"Thank you," I answer, not sure what else to say. My phone buzzes in my pocket, but I don't dare take it out. I can only imagine what Viktor is texting me.

"What brings you to us?" Greg asks.

I look to Zoe for support. "I'm not sure."

"Riley and I met in the library. She shares our fascination with otherworldly creatures."

"I see," the man answers. "What are your opinions on wolves and vamps?"

I don't know how to answer. I choose the answer that will get me to the next level in this group. "If vampires...vamps and wolves exist, they shouldn't. They're an abomination to the world."

The crowd behind me begins shouting agreements and clapping their hands. "Yes, so true."

Greg holds his hands high, and the room goes silent. "Tell us why you believe this, Riley." He smiles a sickening smile, showing a mouth full of rotted teeth.

"I believe my mother was a donneuse...a donor," I remember the story Viktor told me.

"Go on," he urges.

"She gave him her blood in return for money until one day he killed her." Loud gasps echo off the walls. "She left me alone when I was just a child."

"How did it make you feel?" Greg asks.

"Sad, hurt, hungry, unloved." My voice is no louder than a whisper.

"Was it a vampire?" he asks. I nod.

"Do you know who he is?"

"He's dead," I tell the truth. "I watched him die." Zoe looks at me like a proud mother. The crowd behind me goes wild with applause.

"Kill them all," they continue chanting.

Greg stands, opening his arms wide. "Welcome, my child. You are one of us." Does he want me to hug him? Zoe pushes me into his arms from behind, and he wraps me in an awkward embrace. "You are loved," he whispers in my ear. My phone buzzes repeatedly afterward. He steps away. "Come with us tonight."

I look around the room at the congregation that is dressed in all black. "Okay," I answer. The crowd erupts again.

"Get ready, my children. You know what to do." Dear God, this is a cult of crazy people. The congregation separates into small groups that move around the room. Zoe wraps her arm through mine, pulling me with her group.

"Where are we going?" I ask as she pulls me out a back door behind the rest of our group.

"You'll see." My phone buzzes again.

I follow the group into a back alley behind the building and to the main street. Thankfully, I know the French Quarter like the back of my hand. As soon as we hit Bourbon Street, I begin narrating each twist and turn until we stop in front of what looks like a biker bar. A row of motorcycles is parked out front, making a perfect line. I read the name of the bar loud enough for Viktor to hear through the headpiece. "Why are we coming in here? This doesn't look like a vampire hideout."

"Vamps, no. Wolves, yes," Zoe answers.

"These are actual werewolves?" I play dumb.

She smiles. "Yes. And they're just as dumb as you'd think they'd be."

I look around the smoky bar, straight out of the '70s. I'm grateful I don't recognize anyone inside. "Why are we here?"

"We're here to scope it out for the future. If we're lucky enough to be chosen, we'll be their angels." Zoe smiles from ear to ear.

"Their angels?"

"Yes. The ones that will send them to God."

I stare at the delusional girl in front of me. "We're going to kill them?"

"Shh," she covers her mouth with her finger. "We're their angels, silly. We help them be redeemed."

"Zoe, this isn't…"

A tall lycanthrope saunters to our side, and I pray he doesn't recognize *what* I am. "Hello, ladies. To what do we owe the pleasure of your company tonight?"

Zoe giggles. "We're here looking for a good time." Speak for yourself, Zoe.

The wolf looks at me, scanning my body up and down. "I think I can provide just what you need, little lady." He smiles, showing a mouthful of teeth. My phone buzzes again.

"Thank you for the offer, but I'm not interested. I prefer my meat on the darker side if you know what I mean." Zoe laughs at my words. "You know. Sharp, pointy teeth, arrogant, and full of shit."

"This ain't no vamp hangout," the large wolf answers. I've clearly struck a chord.

Zoe slides her hand over his. "What kind of hangout is this?"

The wolf straightens and clears his throat. "It's a place to have a good time and let your claws out a little." The room erupts into howls.

Zoe laughs, straightening her hair. She's in full flirtation mode. "We'll be back soon, I promise." She pulls me toward the door where the rest of the group we came with is waiting.

"I forgot something," I say, turning back into the bar. I walk straight to the wolf she flirted with and turn him to face me. "I need you to look angry as I speak to you. Do you understand?"

"Yes?"

"Good. Edon is your alpha and knows who I am." The wolf turns halfway, spitting on the floor. "Tell Edon to call Viktor. You are in danger. This bar is in danger." The man turns in the other direction. "Do it now."

"Get out of here, bitch," he yells, throwing his hands toward me and the door.

"Good," I whisper, moving toward Zoe and the rest of the crew.

"What did you say to him?" she asks.

"Just reminded him of what kind of trash he is."

Zoe smiles. "Perfect." I follow them out of the bar and back into the street. Unsuspecting humans are walking around, giggling at the posters of half-naked women hanging on the sides of the storefronts and buildings. We turn on to Dauphine, and I whisper the street name for Viktor. I follow them to the door of another bar. This one is much more hidden than the first. There are no motorcycles lined up outside, no evidence of it being anything but a door. The older man in our group pounds on the solid wood entryway. The door cracks open, and a woman answers.

"What?"

"We heard you serve the best gumbo in town."

"Chicken or crawfish?" the woman asks.

"Crawfish. Is there any other way?" The door opens, revealing an older white-haired woman. I don't think she's a wolf, and she's definitely not a vampire. She's dressed in a suit and heels. Not what I expected to be behind the door.

Our group piles in, finding a booth toward the back. This bar reminds me of an antiquated theater. There is a stage, complete with a bright red curtain. When the curtain opens, I'm shocked to find Opie sitting in the middle of the stage. What the hell is going on? I slide back as far as possible into the booth, using shadows to hide my appearance.

"Welcome," Opie says. The crowd murmurs their responses. Opie scans the room until her eyes land on our table. "I sense we have some friends here tonight." I slink back even further, hiding behind Zoe completely. "Don't be fooled by trickery," Opie continues. "Not everything you see is real." The crowd begins to snap. Am I at a poetry slam? "The world around us floats past, ignoring what's right in front of their face. Yet... we're in danger." She pauses while the crowd continues snapping.

"Danger from those who we thought we loved. Danger from those who offer us respite." I angle myself enough to see her. "Danger from those who mean to do us harm." She turns toward the table again.

"We must hide. Blend in. Become one with nature. It's necessary to protect ourselves from those who mean to hurt us." She stands, exiting the stage. As soon as the curtain closes, I slide out of the seat.

"I need to go to the restroom," I whisper to Zoe. I don't know what's going on here, but I want out.

"Amelia. How are you?" Opie steps between me and the door. My phone buzzes several times.

"I'm well, Opie. You?" I stumble over my words. She grabs my arm, pulling me toward the exit.

"You're in danger. Get out now."

"Was that poetry reading for me?" I realize how arrogant that sounds the moment I say it.

"She's here." She pulls me to a back door, shoving me outside in one quick move. "Go, now."

I don't hesitate. I move at fast human speed, pushing my way through the crowd and away from the door. I don't know what the hell that was, but I didn't like it. "Viktor, I'll meet you on the square." My phone buzzes for the millionth time. I don't slow down enough to check it but assume the buzz means he heard me. The further I go, the faster I move. I make it to Jackson Square in record time and walk around, looking for a familiar face. When I see him, I fight the tears threatening to fall.

He wraps both arms around me, pulling me close. "I'm here," he whispers. "Let's go home."

I don't argue as he sweeps me into his car, and we set out across the lake. "Are you okay?" he asks, halfway there.

"I think so. What was that? Did you hear it?"

"I did."

"I think Opie was trying to warn me with her poem."

"Me, too," he answers. "Amelia? Who was there?

"What?"

"Opie said, 'She's here.'" He pauses. "Was she talking about Penelope?"

I turn, facing Viktor. "I think so." His face turns solemn as he grips the gear shift so tightly his knuckles turn white. I lay my hand on top of his, lacing my fingers through his. "I'm sorry." Neither of us makes an effort to pull away until we enter the garage at the Mandeville house. The door flies open, and my little maker runs out at vampire speed.

"Amelia!" she yells, pulling my car door nearly off the hinges. I jump out, dropping to my knees, and wrap my arms around my favorite vampire.

"I missed you, too."

house tour

I SPEND the next few hours in my room, staring out the window. I'm not sure why Opie's words affected me so strongly. Bits of her speech come back to mind, not making any more sense than they did the first time. One line keeps playing through my mind on repeat. *"Not everything you see is real."* What does that mean?

"Amelia?" Celeste knocks on my door. She doesn't wait for me to answer. "Are you okay?"

I smile. "I'm fine. Just a little confused, I guess."

She climbs beside me on the bed. "I'm glad you're back. How was college? Tell me everything." She wraps her tiny hand through my elbow.

"Well, I made a friend. His name is Josh, and his roommate, Roger, convinced him he was a vampire."

Celeste faces me completely.

"Really?"

"He wasn't a vampire, but he convinced Josh he

was. He said his name was Vlad, and he spoke in Old English."

"See, this is why I need to go to college. You don't get this sort of humor from a textbook or the internet."

"I don't think they'd allow you on campus."

Celeste sighs. "It's hard being a thousand years old and trapped in a five-year-old body. My brain isn't five years old."

I've never thought about how hard it must be for her. "You could do online courses."

"Oh, I have. I have three doctoral degrees. One from Harvard, one from Oxford, and one from Tulane." I turn, staring at the immortal child hanging onto my arm.

"Are you joking?"

"Nope. I hold a Ph.D. in psychology, agricultural science, and computer science."

"I worked my butt off for one Ph.D. I can't imagine holding three."

The weight of her head on my shoulder brings comfort. "I've always wanted to live on campus and go to classes. It's different from going online or getting your books through the mail."

"I'm sorry, Celeste."

"Thank you," she whispers. "So, what did you discover?"

"To be honest, I'm not sure. They're definitely bad people, but something seems off. Is Viktor downstairs?"

She shakes her head. "I think he's in his room."

"Do you think it would be okay for me to go in there? I want to talk to him."

Celeste shrugs. "He's grumpy. Good luck." I lean down, kiss her on the forehead, and leave her alone on my bed. Viktor's room isn't far from mine. The large oak door is cracked enough to see inside.

"Viktor?" I call, pushing the door open wider.

He sets a picture down quickly, turning toward the door. "I'm here." I catch a glimpse of red hair in the picture he discarded.

"Are you okay?"

He clears his throat and stands. "Yes, you?"

"I guess. Something about that last building is sticking with me. There's more to this story than the Silver Bullets. That room was full of people who were neither lycan nor vampire, but definitely something."

"It was a coven." Viktor stands from his chair. "And, if Penelope was there, they're all working together under her guise."

"For what purpose?"

"If they're working with the cult, I would guess they have the same goal. To rid the city of wolves and vampires." He leans against a wall, crossing his long legs at the ankle.

"Why would Penelope do that?"

He takes a deep breath. "Penelope was beautiful, smart, and people threw themselves at her feet, no matter what century we were in. She had a way of manipulating you to do her will without anyone ever realizing it. I ignored it because I loved her."

"In modern times, we call it gaslighting."

Viktor laughs. "She always was a trendsetter." He looks up. "To answer your question, if all the wolves and vampires are gone, their system of government and rules will dissipate, making her the one in charge. The city would be her hunting grounds, and there would be no one to stand in her way."

"Then why not go somewhere where she's the only one and become queen of that city? It seems like a lot less work."

"Because that would be boring."

"Don't take this personally, but the more I hear about Penelope, the more I dislike her." I lean against one of the posts from his bed.

"Me, too."

My phone buzzes, and I pull it out of my pocket for the first time since we arrived home. "What the hell?" I flip through the ninety-five messages on my phone. "Are all of these from you?"

He smiles. "Probably. I got a little worried while you were in there."

"Don't drink the Kool-Aid, followed by a laughing face emoji," I read one of the texts out loud.

"It's a reference to Jim..."

"I know what it's a reference to," I interrupt and continue reading. *"I bet his breath smells as bad as the image I see in my mind."* I laugh out loud. "You were actually spot on with that one." I pull the phone up to read another. *"Why do they sound like robots?"*

"They did!" he exclaims. He pulls his phone out of his pocket. "Edon and Oliver are on their way over."

I sigh. "Okay." I turn toward the door.

"Amelia?" I turn toward his voice.

"You did great tonight. I was proud of you." Our eyes lock, and I don't know how to respond. He moves closer to me.

"I don't know how great I did. We don't know any more than we did before. I cut my hair off for nothing."

Viktor takes a piece of my hair into his hand, rubbing it between his fingers. "It'll grow out." On cue, the doorbell rings downstairs. "They're here." He steps back to a respectable distance.

Edon and Ollie are standing in the foyer when we get to the bottom of the stairs. "Good evening," Ollie says. "How did it go?"

"Weirdly," I answer. Viktor and I spend the next thirty minutes explaining everything that happened.

"Thank you for the warning," Edon says. "Mitch called me as soon as you left. I shut them down immediately. In fact, I shut every lycan bar down until further notice."

"That's probably for the best," Viktor adds.

"So, what are we going to do about this?" Oliver asks. "We can't allow this to continue."

"I don't have any intentions of letting that happen."

Viktor's tone has changed from earlier. "I'm not sure I appreciate what you're inferring."

"I can assure you I meant nothing, nor did I mean to infer anything. I simply want to stop this before someone else gets hurt." Ollie is sincere with his answer.

Viktor looks down. "I apologize for being harsh. We're all on edge."

"Amelia needs to go back on campus," Ollie announces.

"Seriously? I've already infiltrated the cult. What's the point? Wasn't that why I was there in the first place?"

"Aye. We need more information. None of us know the next step or how to stop this mess." Ollie slides forward in his seat. "You're our only connection."

"He's right," Viktor adds. "I know you don't want to go back, but I'm afraid it's necessary."

"Okay," I answer. I'm not scared of the cult. I just don't like them. Is that a valid enough reason to not return? Penelope, on the other hand, scares me a little.

"The sun will rise soon. I'll drive you back when you're ready." Viktor walks the two men to the door, and I stand with my arms crossed, like an insolent child.

"You're going back?" Celeste says, coming down the stairs.

"It won't be for long."

She wraps her arms around my waist and sighs. "Be careful."

"I always am," I answer.

Viktor moves next to us. "If you'd like, we can go look for the homes in that picture before you go back."

"Yes! Can we leave now?"

"What picture," Celeste asks.

"I found a picture in the library. It was a young girl, about your age. Something about her seemed familiar. The house she was standing in reminded your dad of homes along the river that used to be there."

"Can I see it?"

"Sure." My backpack is still lying against the stairwell where I laid it when we came inside. I hand her the black-and-white printout.

She studies the print for a while before pulling a magnifying glass out of a cabinet. "See this?" she asks, pointing at something growing behind the girl.

"It looks like grass," Viktor says, receiving a nasty look from his daughter.

"It is a type of grass, but not just any kind. It's called Vetiver and used to be grown near cane fields on oil plantations."

"You think the house in the picture would be a plantation?"

She shrugs. "Could be, or possibly one of the outbuildings from one."

"What's so special about Vetiver?" Viktor asks.

"It's special because it was only grown on the river

during the end of the nineteenth century. It's not known to spread easily. It should still be growing in the same place it was planted." She runs toward the desk where she found the magnifying glass and pulls out an ancient map.

"Here." She points along the river bend, west of the city. "This is where most of it was grown."

Viktor pulls the map closer to his face. "How'd you know this, pumpkin?"

Celeste shrugs. "Google."

He kisses her on the forehead. "You're a genius, little one."

"I know. Let me know what you find."

A few hours later, the sun is high in the sky when Viktor knocks on my door. I've had a hot shower, a clean change of clothes, and styled my mousy brown hair. "Ready to go?" he asks.

"Yep." I open the door and find him wearing a different pair of jeans and a black sweater.

"Look at you, dressing like you're from this century."

He looks down with a smirk. "I thought it was time for an upgrade."

"I don't know if it's an upgrade, but it looks good on you." He motions for me to step in front of him, and I lead the way to the garage and the awaiting SUV.

He opens my door like a modern-age gentleman. "Let's go find some Vetiver."

I laugh at his words. We make our way to a lesser

visited and narrower part of the river. Live oak trees covered in Spanish moss greet us as we drive up the front drive of one of the homes that is still standing. "This is beautiful." In all my years living in New Orleans, I've never seen this part of the city.

"That it is," he agrees. "What exactly are we looking for?"

"I don't know. A picture maybe? Papers?" We enter the front doors of the home.

"Hello!" an older woman greets us. "Are you here for a tour?"

Viktor looks at me for confirmation. "Sure," I answer.

"I was just opening up for the day, but I'd be happy to drag you with me as I get the house ready."

"That sounds perfect." I smile as Viktor places a one-hundred-dollar bill on the counter.

"Oh, no. That's not necessary. I just enjoy sharing the history of this home and the area surrounding it. This way." She leads us from the welcome center area to the interior of the house.

"This home was built by Dr. William Monet in 1789. His family was one of the first to settle in the city." I look at Viktor, curious if he knew of the family. He raises his eyebrows, which doesn't answer my question. She leads us to a large sitting room off the main hallway. "This is where guests would be greeted as they entered the home. There was no air conditioning or heating in those days, so the windows would have been standing open most of the year." She lifts the red cushion bar that keeps visitors from stepping into the room.

"Come this way." She leads us to a smaller room off the back. "This is where we store some of the old photographs. There are too many to display. Several were damaged during the hurricane a few years back, but most are still in great condition." She points to a picture of a smaller house. "This is just one of the many buildings that were once on the property." I glance through each picture, looking for one similar to the picture in my backpack, but finding none.

We follow her into the back sitting room. "This would have been the men's parlor. Male guests would come here to smoke and share news of the city." She leads us up a back set of stairs. "These are the servant stairs. Be careful, they're narrow and uneven," she warns, leading us to four large bedrooms, splitting the hallway. "This would have been the children's bedroom." The room is still decorated like it would have been when the doctor's family lived here. A small, four-post bed sits along the far wall. A toddler bed and an antique baby cradle sit across from it. We follow her down the hall to the last room where a picture hanging in the hallway catches my attention. It's of a little girl with large eyes and dark braids.

"Who's this?" I ask, stopping our private tour.

The woman steps back, studying the picture. "I'm not sure. Since the hurricane, some of the pictures have been replaced by photographs from around the region." She takes the picture off the wall. "I don't know who the girl is, but I've seen her in another photo." She steps across the hallway, opens an old desk, and pulls out an unframed photograph. The woman hands it to me, and I recognize it as the same one I took a screenshot of. "This is the same young lady," she says.

"Do you recognize the building behind her?"

"Let me see." She takes the photo back, studying the image. "It looks quite dilapidated but could be one of the outbuildings that would've been on the other side of the river."

"Are you sure?"

"No." She laughs. "But it looks just like the old photos I've seen before the buildings were destroyed."

"Thank you," Viktor says. "The tour was wonderful." He smiles, and the woman melts slightly.

"Oh," she giggles. "You're quite welcome. Come back anytime." On the way out of the house, he slides the money into a tip jar hanging on the wall next to the door.

"Now what?" I ask, once outside.

"We get you back to campus, and I'll do some research."

I sigh, fastening my seatbelt. "I'm not a fan of that plan."

ELEVEN

creepy professors suck

WE PULL into campus just in time for my history class. Viktor drives me to the front door of the building, where it seems half of the campus is standing around. Stepping out of the car, I close the door at supernatural speed. I hear the window roll down before I make it to the steps of the building.

"Remember to ignore the voices in your head when they tell you to take your clothes off. I don't want to have to deal with the ramifications of that ordeal again." His voice is loud enough for everyone around me to hear. I turn, staring at the ancient vampire. I've never seen his smile this wide before. All eyes are on me as I turn, heading into the building.

Entering the large room, I sit in the same seat as the first day. The minute I walk in, the professor's eyes never leave me. Shit. With everything going on, I forgot about this creep. I look away quickly, not wanting to look interested. Throughout the lesson on Western Civilizations, I notice him watching me. Every few minutes, he makes sure to catch my eye. What's the deal? I pull my phone out, sending a text to Viktor.

> Creepy professor dude is back. Is he possibly a plant?

> Does he have leaves?

> Seriously? Is he a lycanthrope?

> I'll talk to Edon, but I don't think so.

Sliding my phone back into my pocket, I turn, realizing he's standing directly in front of me. He sets a piece of paper on my desk as he continues his lecture. I pretend not to notice, but inside I'm dying to see what it says.

Ten minutes later, class is over. I pack my laptop back into the backpack and open the note. *"Meet me after class"* is scribbled across the top. What now? I sigh, waiting until the rest of the students have left the room before heading to the front.

"You wanted to see me?"

He turns. "Thank you, Riley." He packs his items into an older shoulder bag, hauling it onto his shoulder. "Walk with me."

If I were a normal college freshman, this would be worrisome. I don't question him and follow him out the side door. We walk in silence to a small park area behind the building. "What's going on?" I ask.

He sits on a park bench that surrounds a small rose garden. "What are you?" he asks. I stare at the man, not sure what he's asking.

"I'm not sure what you mean?"

"I think you do." He pulls a notebook and pencil from his bag. "Your skin is pale. Your eyes are very pronounced, and you are wise for your age."

"Thank you?"

He sighs. "Let me explain."

"I think that would be a great idea." My tone is rude, and I don't care.

"I'm a bit of an amateur paranormal investigator and recently have been diving into the world of mythological creatures." He takes a breath and pulls out a copy of my doctoral thesis. "I've been reading some interesting facts, and you fit the bill."

"Where'd you get that book?"

He stuffs my thesis back into his bag. "It's written by someone with a lot more knowledge than you or I. The book opened my mind to things I never realized about creatures living in our city."

"I'm not sure what you think this has to do with me."

"In all my research, I've come across a few mentions of a man I think you're affiliated with." He pulls a small stack of papers from his bag, handing them to me.

Across the top is written Viktor's name. "Do you know him?"

"He's my uncle."

"That leaves us with a little predicament, doesn't it?"

"What are you trying to say? You're wasting my time." I drop the nervous schoolgirl act.

"I'm saying you're either in extreme danger or you're a vampire." I stand, moving into the sunlight. It burns slightly, but not horribly.

"If I were a vampire, would I be able to stand here?" I pull my top lip up. "If I were a vampire, would I have normal teeth?"

"I...I don't know. I've never met a real vampire," he stutters over his words.

"If it's not mentioned in that precious book you have, then why the hell are you asking me if I'm one? That doesn't seem very smart. I'm obviously not a vampire, but if I were, I could rip your arms off before you knew what happened." I step closer. "I could have your body drained of blood within seconds." The professor closes his notebook and clears his throat. "Theoretically, if my uncle was an ancient vampire, confronting his niece in a secluded area wouldn't be the smartest choice."

I move inches from his face and pull on every ounce of vampire blood I have flowing through my veins.

"I think your time is better spent in the classroom, rather than pursuing information that could get you in trouble, or worse." The man is visibly shaking. I look down, realizing the front of his pants are wet. I take the papers from his hands, shredding them in front of him. "Find another hobby, Professor. If not, I'll be forced to speak to my uncle about this."

He turns, moving quickly in the opposite direction, and I take a deep breath. If he's smart, he'll drop whatever insane notion he has planned. He's watched one too many Travel Channel shows.

Took care of the situation.

I send a quick text.

Do I want to know?

It may or may not have involved urine.

Sounds like you're living the full college experience.

I head straight to the library to search for more information on the little girl. "Riley?" a voice calls the moment I sit down at the research computers. I turn to see Zoe, standing a few feet away.

"Where'd you go last night?"

"Oh, I had to go to the bathroom, and then I wasn't feeling well. I just decided to come back here." She moves closer.

"I went to your room. You weren't there."

I laugh awkwardly. "Sleeping. I was sleeping so soundly I must not have heard you outside."

Zoe seems to accept my excuse and sits in the empty seat next to me. "What are you researching?"

"What?"

"These are the old microfiche computers. People don't usually use them unless they're looking for something."

"Just some research for a paper that's due next week in history. What are you doing?"

She scoots closer to me. "What did you think about the meeting?"

"It was interesting," I answer.

"Isn't Greg the best? He's just so...inspiring." I was thinking creepy, but inspiring works too.

I slide my chair back, scrapping it against the tile floor. "Zoe, you mentioned something about angels last night."

"Not real angels," she interrupts. "Well, in a way they're real, I guess." Her eyes take on a glassy look. "We become angels of death if we're chosen."

"How are you chosen?"

She shrugs. "Greg decides. When it's your time, it's glorious." My mind flashes back to Meredith and the aftermath that followed. Is that what she was? An angel, chosen by Greg?

"What was the last place we went to?"

"The poetry slam?" I nod. "It's a safe place where like-minded people come together."

"Like-minded?"

"You know. The ones who think like us. The ones who want them all dead."

"What if I don't want them dead?" I ask.

Zoe stands, sliding her chair under the desk. "Then this conversation is over."

"Wait." I put my hand on her arm. "I don't know what to believe. I'm confused."

"There's another poetry slam tonight. Why don't you come."

"I'll think about it," I answer as she walks away.

I gather my belongings without doing any research and find the nearest bus stop. I need to talk to Opie.

An hour and a smelly city bus trip later, I walk into her shop off the square. "Just a minute," she calls from the back. I don't wait, I head straight back, past the curtain.

"Amelia?" she stops what she's doing and stares.

"Ophelia?" I return her energy. "Tell me what the hell's going on." She rushes past me and locks the front door of the store. I watch as she pulls the shades down and turns off the lights.

"What are you doing here?"

"I need answers, and you're the only one who can give them to me." She pulls me past the curtain into the back of the store. "What do you want to know?"

"Were you trying to tell me something last night?"

She sighs. "I would think it was obvious. I told you to get out of there. You were in danger."

"Was I really in danger?"

Opie crosses her hands across her chest. "Why else would I tell you to leave?"

I shrug. "It seems to be the trend lately. Was Penelope there?"

Her eyes grow. "Yes."

"Why?"

"She's working with the coven."

"Why were you there?"

"Because I'm working with the coven, too," she answers.

"You're a witch. Is that your coven?" My words offend her.

"I am not a witch. Don't get me confused with them. I am a voodoo priestess. I would think you would remember that since you tried to get me to bring your friend back to life."

"Why would a voodoo priestess, a witches coven, and an ancient vampire work together?"

"I think you know," she whispers, blowing something in my face and the world goes dark.

......

My eyes open to a dark room. My arms and legs are bound, along with a gag in my mouth. Well, this sucks. I wait for my eyes to adjust and realize I'm still in Opie's shop. The lights are off, and I'm alone. My backpack and phone are sitting on her seance table along with a note. I easily break the ties around my wrists and ankles and pick up the note.

Sorry, but this is for your own good. Stay away from the coven.

The note reads. The front of the store is dark, and any signs of life are gone. What the hell just happened?

> Can you meet me at Jackson Square?

I send a quick text.

> Did they move Tulane?

I send the middle finger emoji. My phone buzzes within minutes.

> I'm still in town. Is everything okay?

> I'll meet you in front of the cathedral.

Minutes later, he's at my side. "Did something happen?"

"I went to visit Opie."

"You what? Why would you do that alone?"

I sigh. "I don't know, Dad. Don't tell Mom."

Viktor smirks at my words. "Someone is a little snarky."

"To answer your question, I wanted to ask her about last night."

"I'm guessing by the rope that's still tied around your wrists, that she wasn't a fan of the question."

I shake my head. "She knocked me out with some kind of powder. When I woke up, she was gone."

"Amelia, why would you do that alone?"

"Because I wanted to ask about Penelope, and I didn't want to put you in that situation." I sigh, moving away from the crowd. "I know talking about her is hard for you, and I was trying to keep you from having to do it."

Viktor's eyes soften. "Thank you, but I can assure you I'm over her."

"No, you're not. No matter how hard you try to convince me or yourself that you are, you're not. You're still in love with her. I was trying to protect you."

He looks at his boots. "I don't need protecting."

"It's what I do. Get used to it. I protect the ones I care about." The words are out of my mouth before I have time to think them through. Where did that come from? Do I care for him?

Viktor picks my hand up from my side and gently unties the rope still attached. "I protect the ones I care about, too."

zoe

MINUTES LATER, we're walking into my campus dorm. "I wonder if that lovely young lady, Samantha, will be here?" He smirks at his words.

"It won't be long until we find out." We open the stairwell door and find Samantha standing inches away from the door. I have a hard time controlling my laughter at the irony.

"Good afternoon, Mr. Smith," she says. She's wearing a crop top that's more crop than top. Knit shorts hang low on her hips.

"Good afternoon, Samantha." He lifts her hand to his lips, kissing gently. I swear her knees sway slightly. "You're looking quite lovely today."

Samantha giggles, twisting her hair between her fingers. "Thank you for noticing." She rubs her fingers along her belly button ring, pulling the waistband of her shorts down slightly. "I wonder if you could help me with something in my room?"

Viktor looks to me for help. "I'm sorry, Samantha. I need Uncle Vik to help me move a dresser. Can he take a rain check?"

"Maybe when you finish helping Riley?" she asks him. I don't exist in her eyes at the moment.

"Samantha!" I clap my hands loudly. She turns toward me for the first time. "He's not going to come to your room. He's not going to help you move anything around, and he's especially not going to accidentally fall with his penis landing inside of you! Excuse us, please."

The girl stares at me like I've lost my mind. "I wasn't..." she pauses.

"You weren't what? Throwing yourself at my uncle who's clearly much older than you and not interested."

She sighs, turning away. Viktor's laugh is low as we enter my room. "Is it possible to fall and my penis land inside of someone? I don't recall that happening before."

"All the time. It's a dangerous world out there for penises." Is that right? Penisi? Peens? Penisess? Whatever.

"I'll keep that in mind." Viktor laughs. "Isn't it time for English?"

I check the clock above my door. "Yes, but I'm not going. I already did my homework and turned it in." A loud knock on my door makes me jump. I roll my eyes in anticipation of who's going to be standing outside.

"Samantha! He's not..." I'm surprised to see Josh instead of Samantha. "Oh, hi!"

"Hi." He waves. He's holding a dozen white roses. "These are for you." He hands me the glass vase.

"That wasn't necessary, but thank you." I take the beautiful roses.

"They're not from me. I mean, I can buy you some if you want, but it might be a while until I have enough money."

"No, that's fine. I just assumed they were from you."

Josh shrugs. "I found them on the desk downstairs."

"Thank you for bringing them to me." Josh smiles and turns without saying anything else. "Are these from you?" I ask my "uncle."

"They can be," Viktor answers. I pull the card from the envelope. "What's it say?"

I read the poem written in beautiful script.

"We loved with a love that was more than love."

I flip the card over, looking for clues as to who they're from. "What does this mean?"

"It's from Poe's poem, *Annabel Lee.*"

"Poe, as in Edgar Allan Poe? Who would send me a

dozen white roses with a nearly two-hundred-year-old poem written on the card?" He takes the card, inspecting the handwriting.

"I don't like this." Viktor hands it back to me. "I think it's better for you to come to the house tonight."

"A dozen white roses and a beautiful card are nothing to be concerned about," I argue.

"Normally, no. But whoever sent those knows where you are and knows you by Riley instead of Amelia."

"Maybe they're from the psycho history professor. He wasn't the sharpest pencil in the box. Maybe I didn't scare him as much as I thought I did."

"I don't think he did this." Viktor sits on the edge of my bed. "I think these are from Penelope."

I look up at her name. "Penelope? Why would she send this to me?"

"To let you know she's aware of where you are and what you're doing. It's all about control with her. It's a warning."

"If she was going to try to hurt me, she would've done it by now. Hell, she could've killed me at Opie's store a year ago. Instead, she walked right past me and left without another word."

Viktor scratches his head. A very human movement. "I don't like it," he repeats.

I decide to change the subject. "I was invited to another poetry slam by Zoe."

"When?"

"It's tonight."

He sighs, walking around my room. "This can't be a coincidence. Are you thinking of going?"

"I haven't decided."

He steps inches in front of me. "I don't want you going in there alone."

"You can't go. If Penelope *is* there, she'll spot you in seconds."

"Maybe I could conceal my appearance."

"Viktor, stop. I'm an immortal, not a helpless little human that needs round-the-clock protection. I'll be fine."

He sighs. "What about Ollie? He won't be known around town. No one will recognize him as a vampire."

"Fine. If it makes you feel better, ask him." It makes me feel better too, but I'm not willing to admit that to Viktor.

"He said he'll meet us in the lobby after class." Viktor keeps his head down, staring at his phone blankly.

I gently lift his chin, forcing him to look at me. "Everything's going to be alright." He slides his palm against my cheek, gently rubbing his thumb along my jawline.

"Do you promise?"

"I promise." Feeling the tension between us rise, I turn, hoping to escape the desire forming in the pit of my stomach. Simmer down, stomach. We don't have feelings for Viktor. He's just a friend. The butterflies aren't listening and are in full flight around the pits of my insides. I clear my throat before speaking. "Class should be just about over."

Viktor seems to gain his wits and stands up straighter than before. "After you, mon amour."

A year ago, his pet name for me filled my body with dread. Now, they add to the turmoil brewing inside. I ignore it and head downstairs, hoping we don't run into Samantha again. Luckily, she's nowhere to be seen as we enter the empty downstairs common room.

True to his word, Ollie is sitting on the stairs leading to the front door. He stands as we exit. "Good afternoon," he says, with gentlemanly charm. "You missed class today, Riley."

"Riley didn't do her homework, but Amelia figured the two-hundred-page thesis she turned in would do the trick."

Ollie smirks. "It was a little overkill. All I requested was a one- or two-page essay."

"Consider it my homework for the entire semester."

He smiles. "Do you have any information?"

I share information about the cult, the poetry slam, Opie, and the roses. Ollie is quiet during the entire explanation, listening intently to every word until the end. "I agree with Viktor. The flowers are not a coincidence. Especially with what happened at the poetry slam. Do you think Penelope was the one Ophelia was warning you about?"

I glance at Viktor before answering. "I do. I'm not sure what their dynamic is, but there's something between the two of them. I'm going to the meeting tonight."

Ollie looks between the two of us. "Are you sure that's smart?"

I sigh loudly. "No, but if we want to get to the bottom of this mess, I don't have a choice."

"Would you accompany her?" Viktor asks Oliver.

"Are you okay with that?" Ollie asks me.

I shrug. "Sure. As long as you remember, you're there *with* me, not to rescue me. I'm not helpless." I make eye contact with both of them.

"Understood," Ollie answers. "I'm there purely as an observer. When do we leave?"

"I'll get in touch with Zoe and find out the details. You might want to change." Ollie glances down at his clothes.

"Why?" He's wearing a pair of perfectly pressed khakis and an argyle cardigan.

"You look like an English professor," I tease.

"I *am* an English professor."

I text Zoe, and she responds quickly with the address. The poetry slam is at the same place as last night, which surprises me. I don't know why I expected them to move locations daily. Guess they're not as secretive as I thought.

Viktor has conveniently stayed in the city since I decided to attend the meeting. He's been scrolling through social media for the past hour while hanging out in the common room. Secretly, I'm happy he's stayed. I enjoy having him nearby. "What?" he asks, looking up from his phone. "You're staring at me."

"Am I? Sorry. I was lost in thought."

"About?" He slides his phone into his pocket.

Shit. I decide to lay it on the line. "What are we?"

He wrinkles his forehead in confusion, looking around the room. "Vampires," he whispers.

I laugh out loud. "No. What are *we*? Are we friends? Because if we are, I don't know when that really happened. We were more like parents who lived in the same house and tolerated each other for the sake of the child. Now...I enjoy your company."

Viktor smiles at my admission. "You do?"

"Not that much. Don't get excited." It's his turn to laugh.

"To answer your question, I'd like to think we're friends. I enjoy your company, and my daughter loves you very much."

Thinking of Celeste brings a smile to my face. "I love her, too."

"If I let something happen to you, she would have my head, literally. I'm here purely to ensure my livelihood."

I laugh. "I need to change for the meeting." I head upstairs, passing Samantha on her way down.

"Is your uncle down there?" God, she has some wicked radar.

"I don't know. Last I saw him, he was passed out drunk." I keep moving, heading straight to my room. I change into a pair of skintight leather pants, a black sweater, and a halter. Badass Amelia is back.

Ollie and Viktor are both surfing the web when I come back down. Ollie has changed into jeans and a fitted Henley shirt. Samantha is nowhere in sight, and I'm curious to know why, but not curious enough to ask. "Ready?" I ask, pulling them away from their phones.

Viktor stares at me. "Cat Woman called. She wants her clothes back."

"Do you actually know who Cat Woman is?" I retort.

He wiggles his eyebrows. "Personally." He smiles. "Here, put this in your ear." Viktor hands me another earpiece.

"I can handle myself," I remind him.

"I know, but this is for emergencies." I slide the earpiece in, glaring at him the whole time.

Oliver and I drive separately and park a few blocks away from the building. "Are you ready?" he asks, checking our surroundings.

"As I'll ever be." I slide out of the passenger seat and my phone buzzes.

Be safe.

I will.

I knock loudly on the door, and the same woman answers. "What?"

Pulling out my phone, I read the text from Zoe. "Do you sell jambalaya?"

"With or without hot sauce?" the woman asks.

"Can you eat it without hot sauce?" I slide my phone back into my pocket as the door opens.

"Come in," the woman beckons. We enter the smokey room, finding it just as full as last night.

"Riley!" Zoe waves from across the room. "Dr. Fitzgerald?" Shit. I didn't think about a student recognizing him.

"I hope you don't mind that I brought a friend. Dr. Fitzgerald shares the same values as we do. I've known him since I was a little girl."

Zoe checks Ollie from head to toe. "Sure." She smiles. "He needs to meet Greg. He has the final say."

"Of course," I agree. We slide into the seat next to her. "What time does it start?"

"Could be any minute, could be in hours." Zoe shrugs.

"Hey, Riley," a familiar voice says, coming to our table.

I stare at Violet, not sure what to call her or why she's here. "It's me, Stacey. We're in Psychology together."

"Of course! Stacey. How are you?" My phone buzzes.

"I'm good. I met Aria," she points to a young girl a few tables away, "today at a deli. We got to talking, and she invited me to come tonight." She turns toward Ollie. "Hello, Dr. Fitzgerald."

"Stacey." He smiles. "Care to join us?" She slides into the seat beside him. My phone continues to buzz. Like last time, I'm going to have a million texts to sift through.

The room goes dark, and a woman walks on stage. It's not Opie, and I'm slightly disappointed. We spend the next few hours listening to at least ten different poets give their renditions of life in New Orleans. The poems they read are just that, poems. No warnings or worries. "Ladies and gentlemen, thank you for coming tonight and supporting local artists." The room erupts into applause, and the crowd gets up to leave.

"Is that it?" I ask Zoe.

"Did you like it?" she asks.

"I did, but it was different from last night." Zoe shrugs, sliding out of the booth. I wrap my arm around Violets as we head toward the door with Ollie in tow. "Why are you here?" I whisper.

"I was invited," she whispers back. "Someone sent me a bouquet of white roses today with an invitation attached."

Ollie pulls me to a stop at the same time the room

goes black. "Thank you for coming, ladies and gentle-men," a voice says over the speaker system.

"Move," Ollie's voice whispers in my ear. I don't hesitate to follow instructions. The three of us move at superhuman speed through the door and down the block. Humans give us a wide berth as we barrel past them.

"What the hell was that?" Violet asks once we're clear of the building.

"Penelope," Oliver and I answer in unison.

"What's her deal? Is this some sort of game to her?"

I pull my phone out of my pocket, reading the last message from Viktor.

> I'm going inside. I need to see if it's her.

"Shit!" I yell, running back toward the bar.

Oliver and Violet are right on my heels as we make it back to the bar in record time. I slam open the door, nearly pulling it off the hinges. The room is still dark, and my eyes adjust quickly. "What's going on?" Ollie asks as he and Violet flank either side of me.

"Viktor," I answer. "He came in here looking for Penelope."

Somehow in the few seconds it took to leave and come back, the room is empty. Drinks are still sitting on the table, and Lo-Fi Jazz is still playing in the background, but the humans that occupied the room moments earlier are gone. "Where is everyone?" Violet asks.

"Gone," Viktor says, coming from a back room. "The whole damn building is empty."

"They were just here." Ollie looks as confused as I feel.

"Penelope?" I ask Viktor.

"Gone, too."

The door opens, flooding the room with artificial light. "She said you'd return." Zoe is standing in front of the now closed door. Strapped to her chest is a strangely shaped vest.

"Zoe? What is that?"

She smiles a sickly smile. "I've been chosen."

Viktor looks at me for answers I don't have time to give. "Zoe, please. Don't do this." I realize what's strapped to her chest. "You won't just destroy yourself and this building, you'll destroy the lives of innocent humans."

"Shut up, bloodsucker."

"Amelia?" Viktor warns.

"Zoe, please. Don't do this. It's not worth it." I've only known the girl a few days but watching her die and kill innocent people in hopes of killing us is not something I want to witness.

"We have to go," Violet warns.

"I can't leave her." I step toward the girl.

"You can't save her," Viktor's words are harsh.

"It's happened, Riley. Greg chose me. I'm one of the

angels." Zoe lifts something that resembles a button high in the air.

"No!" I scream as arms wrap around me, pulling me to the back of the building and into a nearby alley. An explosion rattles my eardrums as the building behind us bursts into flames and splinters. Viktor, Oliver, Violet, and I fall to the ground as the impact waves shove us forward. Screams and alarms fill my ears with the sounds of the horror she just inflicted.

THIRTEEN

i miss being human

THE WORLD around me is in shambles. Sirens echo through the Quarter, and my mind repeats the events that led to this. Zoe and who knows how many more are dead because of a useless cause for a useless leader. The four of us have made our way a few streets over, but the screams and chaos that ensued can still be heard, even from here.

"What was that?" Oliver asks. "Why would she take her own life?"

"Because in her confused mind, sacrificing her life was payment for taking out four vampires," I answer.

"How'd she know you were a vampire?" Viktor asks a great question.

I shrug. "Maybe she's known the entire time. Maybe this whole damn thing was a setup from the beginning. Maybe Penelope has been one step ahead of us the whole time."

He stops moving, leaning against a brick building. "More like ten steps ahead. She's had two hundred years to plan whatever the hell this is."

"How'd I get dragged into it?" Violet asks, crossing her arms in front of her chest.

"Harrison was your maker," Viktor answers. "She's trying to rid the city of anyone who isn't her."

"She wasn't alone," I remind them all. "Yes, Penelope is the mastermind, but Greg is the one pushing the buttons. He's managed to brainwash dozens of people just like Zoe. As long as they're still around and he's in charge, there will be more of these. More senseless deaths. We have to stop them. Without Greg or the cult, Penelope will be forced to fight her own battles."

"I agree," Oliver says. "Without their help, she'll be forced to retreat and rethink her attack."

"Zoe was my only connection to them. Plus, apparently, they know I'm a vampire. I can't very well show up at the next meeting and be welcomed into Greg's arms."

"No, but your friend Josh can." I look up at Viktor's words.

"I can't do that to him. He was terrified of Roger when he thought he was a vampire. Do you think he'd actually walk into a cult meeting and not break out in hives?"

"Who is Josh?" Violet asks.

I sigh. "He's a kid in my dorm that is very sweet and naive."

"Sounds like he's perfect for the job."

"What if something happens to him?" I persist.

"It won't. We'll make sure of it," Viktor answers.

"You can't guarantee that. I couldn't save Zoe. I won't put Josh in that kind of situation."

"He's our only chance," Violet adds. "I don't know him, but I understand your trepidation, especially after what just happened. But you're right. We have to stop the cult, and we need a foot in the door."

"Shit. Okay. But he has to know the truth. We can't send him in there blindly."

It's Viktor's turn to sigh. "Do you think he can handle the truth? You saw how well it went when he thought his roommate was a vampire."

"It's the only way I'll agree to this whole thing. He has to know the truth, and he has to understand the ramifications." I stand my ground against the ancient vampire, staring me down. Viktor holds up his hands in surrender. "I think it's better if I talk to him alone."

"I'm sorry about Zoe," Viktor says as we pull in front of the dorm.

"Yeah, me too. I've never felt so helpless. There was nothing I could do to save her, was there?"

He sets his hand on top of mine and squeezes. "No. You did everything you could."

"If Josh agrees to join this cult, then what?"

"Then we end Greg." I look down at our joined hands.

"Thank you for getting me out of there. I know it was you who grabbed me."

Viktor smiles, squeezing my hand again. "The blast most likely wouldn't have killed you, unless it managed to decapitate you or pierce your heart with a flying piece of wood, but it would've hurt like a son of a bitch." His words make me laugh for the first time since the explosion.

"You're such an asshole." I close the car door behind me, and my phone buzzes.

> The word ass triggers me.

> Good!

I send a GIF of a donkey smiling and hear him laugh through the open window before heading inside the dorm. I consider procrastinating but decide to get it over with and go straight to Josh's door. The boy that opens the door isn't what I remember. His hair is blonde, and he looks like an average American college kid. When he sees me, his eyes grow twice their size.

"Hi." He smiles wide. "I've done what you asked. See?" He runs his hands up and down his body. "I washed the dye from my hair and have been wearing my normal clothes. Did you tell them I was just pretending?"

"I did, and they wanted me to tell you that you're doing well and that they've been watching. I'm actually here for another reason today. I need to see Josh. Is he around?" Roger's stance relaxes, and he clears his throat.

"He's eating at the commons." He pulls his phone out. "He should be back any minute. Want me to text him?"

"No, thank you. Will you tell him to come to my room when he gets back?"

"Um, yes, but he's not allowed on your floor."

I smile my best smile. "I'm not allowed on *this* floor." Roger sticks his head out of the door, looking down both sides of the hallway.

"Good point. I'll tell him."

"Thanks."

I head upstairs and collapse on the bed. The events of the past few hours weigh heavily on my mind. Zoe's eyes flash to mind. The first day I met her, she looked normal. Today, she looked crazed. Her pupils were dilated, and her mind was scattered. Could she have been drugged? A knock on my door draws me from my thoughts. I open the door to see Josh standing on the other side.

"Roger said you wanted to see me," he whispers.

"Come in." I open the door wide. "Have a seat."

Josh looks skeptical as he slides into the desk chair in the corner of the room. "What's up?"

I sit back on the bed before speaking. "How long have you lived in New Orleans?"

He flips his wrist around, looking at an invisible watch. "In three days, it will be eight months."

"What do you think about the city?"

He shrugs. "I like it. Why?"

I sigh, not sure how to go about saying any of this. "What is your opinion of vampires? Do you believe in them?"

Josh stands from the chair. "Did Roger put you up to this? Is he starting that crap again?"

"No, it's not about Roger. I'm asking a serious question. Do you think they really exist?"

"I dated a girl once that believed in them. She read some books that were all about vampires and insisted on calling me by one of their names for a while." He looks down. "I don't know if I actually believe or not."

"What if I told you they were real?"

"I'd poop my pants."

I smile at his naivety. "What if I told you they're like humans? Just like there are good and bad humans, there are good and bad vampires." He doesn't respond, just stares. "There are people out there that want to hurt or kill the good ones because of what they believe through prejudice."

"What about the bad ones?"

"Believe it or not, there are more good than bad."

"Then, I don't know what I would think. Every movie or television show I've ever watched paints them as horrible killers."

I nod. "Hollywood has a way of doing that. Good vampires don't sell tickets."

"What are you trying to tell me, Riley? Are you a vampire?"

"What if I said yes?"

He moves toward my refrigerator. "Then this would make sense." He opens the door to my bottles of blood. "I found them when I stayed in your room."

"You didn't say anything."

"What would I say? Hey, Riley, found your blood?"

I laugh. "Yeah, I guess that wouldn't have worked."

"Why now? Why are you telling me the truth now?"

"Because we need your help."

Josh sits back down. "Have you met me, Riley?"

"Amelia," I correct him. "My name is Amelia, not Riley. To answer your question, yes, I am a vampire. I'm a baby vampire, but nevertheless, a vampire."

To his credit, Josh doesn't run out of the room. He stares at me for longer than usual. "What kind of help do you need?"

I smile. "There's a group of people in the city trying to kill us. I went to a couple of meetings, thinking they didn't know who or what I was. Now, I know they do."

"You need me to go to the meetings?" he asked, putting the puzzle pieces together.

"Yes. They're evil. They have to be stopped before more people die."

He pulls a folded paper from his pocket. "I found this in our room." He turns the paper around to show me. It's a flyer, advertising a "spiritual revolution" in the French Quarter. "Is this the group?"

I nod. "They're the ones responsible for the explosion in the Quarter today."

Josh pulls his phone out. "The news is saying it was a gas leak. I saw an article on it earlier."

"It wasn't a gas leak." I look down, not sure how much I should share.

He's silent for a while. "This paper belongs to Roger. He got it from someone in his music appreciation class. I'll ask him if I can attend with him."

"Thank you, Josh."

He smiles. "No one has ever asked me to do something like this before. I kind of feel important."

"You are important," I answer. "When does the flyer say the next meeting is?"

He scans over the paper. "It doesn't, but I'm sure Roger will know. He told me he was going. He's gone from pretending to be a vampire, to an activist. I don't know what you did to him, but you scared the poop out of him."

"Maybe we scared him too much?"

"Nah, he deserved it." He stands, heading toward the door. "I'll let you know if there's a meeting tonight."

"After what happened today, I imagine they'll lay low for a few days. We'll have an earpiece for you to wear when they do meet again. I don't want to put you in danger. The earpiece will let us know what's going on and, if you get in trouble, come to your rescue.

Josh smiles. "I kind of feel like James Bond."

"Just like James Bond," I answer. I watch him leave, feeling a knot form in the pit of my stomach.

"I won't let anything happen to you," I whisper as the door closes.

He agreed to do it.

I text Viktor.

Good. Are you okay?

No.

I answer truthfully, stuffing the phone back into my pocket. If I were human, I'd crawl under my covers and sleep the anger, hurt, and frustration away. Sleep was always an escape from reality. Now, even that's gone. Instead, I head toward the shower, washing away the dirt from the explosion, along with everything else.

God, I miss my fucked up, excuse for a life. For the first time in a year, I wish to be human again.

FOURTEEN

exploring ruins

THE CAMPUS IS asleep as I wander through the darkened halls. My phone buzzed several times, but I ignore the texts. I don't want to talk to anyone right now. Is there any reason for me to stay on campus? No. Do I have anywhere else to go? Again, no.

I leave Tulane and walk the four miles to the Quarter. I miss the days when I could walk around and be invisible. Now, everyone stares. I think back to how many vampires or lycan I must have passed on these same streets over the years. Probably hundreds. Hell, even thousands.

I pass Opie's shop. The windows are filthy, showing no signs of life. Did she shut down? I keep moving, passing several ghost tours on the way, until I reach a familiar house on Royal Street. The house where this whole mess started. I stare at the now abandoned home, remembering my first meeting with Viktor and how Harrison "saved" me.

I continue walking, moving out of the Quarter and toward the Garden District. Turning the corner toward what used to be Harrison's house, I catch a glimpse of movement behind me. I pull back into the bushes, making sure I didn't imagine it. Whatever I saw stopped and steps out of the light. I can tell whoever's following me is human. What kind of idiot is dumb enough to follow a vampire? I step completely out of the light and head straight toward my stalker. Faster than human eyes can track, I'm behind them with my arm wrapped around their neck.

"Why are you following me?" I spew.

"I...I wanted to see where you were going." I recognize the voice immediately.

"Josh?" I pull back, and he steps into the light, allowing me to see his face. "What the hell? I could've killed you. What were you thinking?"

"For the first time in my life, I feel important." He runs a hand through his hair. "God, this is dumb." He sighs. "I've never been important. When you asked me to go to the meeting to help you all, I didn't want that feeling to end. I'm sorry, I know how stupid I sound."

Stepping back, I look at the young boy. "Yes, it was extremely stupid, but I know how you feel. I grew up the same way."

"You're a vampire, which makes you very important. How could you possibly know how I feel?" I laugh at his admission.

"Important? No. Just immortal." I look at the looming house in front of me. "My friend lives here. Would you like to meet her?"

"Sh...sure," he stumbles over his words. "Is she like you?"

"If you're asking if she's a vampire, then yes. But she's nothing like me." Josh follows me to the front door of the familiar home. Two knocks later, Violet opens the door.

"Amelia? Did something happen?"

"No. I was wandering around the city and discovered I had someone following me." I step aside, revealing Josh.

"Hello?" He waves. "I'm Josh."

"Hello, Josh." She sticks her hand in front of her. "Violet." She turns toward me, recognizing his name. "Are you the same Josh that's going to help us?"

He smiles widely. "Am I?" he asks me.

"That's up to you," I answer.

"Come in." Violet opens the door wide. Josh walks in wide-eyed.

"This is beautiful. I've never been inside a home like this before."

"I'm in the midst of remodeling," Violet says. "Would you care for anything to drink?"

"Like a human drink? I don't want any blood if that's what you mean."

Violet laughs. "I have soft drinks, water, and even a bit of alcohol. What would you like?"

"Oh, Coke is fine. I'm not old enough to drink alcohol yet."

"Of course." Violet leaves the room, returning moments later, carrying a cold bottle of Coca-Cola, and handing it to him. "Why were you following our friend Amelia?"

"It's dumb," he answers shyly.

"He was bored," I answer for him, trying to save him the embarrassment.

"How long have you been a...a vampire? If you don't mind me asking."

Violet sits on the couch, patting the spot next to her. "Almost a hundred years." His eyes grow wide as he sits. "This house belonged to my maker. It's mine now." She doesn't elaborate on information he doesn't need to know.

"Maker?" he asks.

"The one who turned me into a vampire."

"So, kind of like your parent?" My mind flashes to my five-year-old "parent" who is probably giving Viktor hell about my whereabouts right now.

"You could think of it like that."

Josh looks around the finely decorated room. "This isn't what I thought a vampire's home would look like."

"Did you expect coffins hanging everywhere?" Violet asks.

"I guess I did." He raises his Coke bottle in the air.

"Thank you for the drink, Violet. It was nice to meet you." He turns toward me. "I'm sorry I followed you. I'll leave you two alone." He heads toward the door.

"You're going to walk back to the dorm?" I ask.

He shrugs. "Yeah. I don't have money for an Uber."

"Nonsense. I'll take you. Is my car still here?"

Violet smiles. "The key is in the ignition."

Minutes later, we enter the garage, finding my antique Nissan just like I remember. I don't know what Violet did to it, but it's gorgeous and starts immediately. Josh slides into the passenger seat. "This car doesn't match the house."

I laugh out loud. "That's the understatement of the night." Luckily, traffic is light, and it doesn't take long to get back to campus. Josh is quiet the entire trip, staring out the window, apparently deep in thought.

I find a spot in the back of the dorm parking lot and back in like a pro. "A penny for your thoughts?"

He laughs. "Honestly, they're not worth a penny. I'm just thinking about how much bigger the world is than I realized." He holds the door open for me, and we enter the dorms together. "Good night, Ril...Amelia."

"Good night, Josh. Let me know as soon as you have a date and time." He nods, and we go our separate ways. I pull my phone out, reading through the small number of texts I ignored. One, in particular, grabs my attention.

> What happened today? Daddy won't tell me.

I stare at the message from my maker. How would she have heard about the explosion?

> There was an explosion. We're all okay.

> Promise?

> Pinky promise.

Tears fill my eyes. Celeste is the only person I've ever truly loved. I don't remember loving my mother as much as I love her.

> I miss you.

I add another message.

> Come home.

Her words tear at my heartstrings.

> I will, soon. I promise.

According to the clock on my phone, it's only a few hours until sunrise. I stare at the ceiling above my bed, picturing all the possible outcomes of this insanity until the sounds of chirping make their way through my window. What am I supposed to do? Go to class? No. I pick up my backpack, and the picture I found in the library falls to the floor. With everything that's happened, I completely forgot about it.

> Skipping class. Want to go search for more information on the picture of the girl?

I send a text to Viktor, my friend. That sounds weird to say, even in my head.

> I'm currently in time-out but can escape and be there in thirty minutes.

I laugh, picturing Celeste punishing him for not sharing more information with her. By the time I change into clothes that match my attitude, my phone buzzes letting me know Viktor is here. I head downstairs, finding him in his normal parking spot, the fire lane. I climb into the passenger seat, throwing my backpack in the back.

"Hey!" a tiny voice yells. I jump from my seat, opening her door at vampire speed.

"Celeste!" She jumps into my arms. "You're a sight for sore eyes."

"I made Daddy bring me."

"She's not lying. It's the only way she would let me leave. I thought the three of us could spend the day together."

I smile, setting her back on the ground. "I think that's exactly what I need." We climb inside and strap in.

"So where are you wanting to go for more research?" Viktor asks, pulling away from the curb.

"Anywhere that's not in this city." He pulls us away from Tulane and out of the Crescent City.

"I found a few places that might still be growing Vetiver," Celeste announces from the back seat. She hands me a list of addresses close to the river. "I put them in Daddy's phone earlier."

"You're a genius." I take the list from her.

"I know. Just click on his maps app, and we can go to the first one." I follow directions and hook the map into Viktor's car display.

"Is that how that works?" he asks, staring at the map that appears on the screen.

"There's more on your phone than TikTok, Dad." I laugh at her words. Viktor follows the directions to a T, pulling us in front of the burned-out ruins of a historic home. Five two-story pillars, a brick porch floor, and a fireplace are the only thing that remains.

"This is beautiful." I step out of the car.

"And creepy," Celeste adds.

"And creepy," I agree. "What do you expect to find?"

"Well, I did some research on the home that used to be here. It was owned by the DuPont family."

"Are they related to THE DuPont family?"

"I guess," she answers. "Let's look for the grass."

"Okay, you're the expert."

She smiles. "It's about time my genius is recognized." She laughs, imitating an evil character from a cartoon. "Follow me."

We walk the perimeter of the remains, and Celeste finds several spots where the grass is still growing. None of them share any resemblance to the photograph. "I don't think this is the right place," I announce after walking at least five miles.

"Yeah, me either. Let's go to the next one." We load the car, and I pull up the directions to the next location on the screen.

Ten minutes later, we pull into an empty field. "Are you sure this is it?" I ask to the back seat.

"The GPS coordinates are right." She pulls her phone out, double-checking our location. "I thought there'd be *something* still standing." Celeste slides to the front of her seat, trying to see something.

"Most of these homes are long since gone," Viktor says, "either burned or ruined by hurricanes." He stops at a beautiful view overlooking the river.

"My cell service is spotty, but according to the *Historical Sites of Orleans Parish* website, this home belonged to the Chambers family. They grew tobacco and cotton and weren't very nice people."

"What do you mean?" I ask, picking a beautiful purple flower from the ground.

"The family was known for their cruelty. This

article doesn't go into detail, but I imagine we don't want to know. Look, here's a picture of Mr. Chambers."

She hands me the phone, and my heart drops. "Viktor. Look at this."

Viktor studies the picture, enlarging it enough to see details. "That bastard," he whispers. The man in the pictures looks just like Harrison, standing in front of a house that has long since been destroyed.

"Do you think it's really him?" I ask.

"I'm not aware of him living here, but I wouldn't put it past him to own the land. He had land throughout the parish."

"What am I missing?" Celeste asks.

"Look closely at the photograph, mon petit amour." Celeste takes the phone back, studying the picture.

"Is that...is that Harrison?" She swipes through a few more photos, finding another one of him. "It's definitely him," she announces. "Here he is with some children."

"Are they immortal children?" Viktor asks.

"I don't think so." She hands me her phone again. A young girl standing beside Harrison catches my attention. I pull the photograph out of my pocket, matching the two together.

"Oh, my God. Viktor, look. It's the girl from the picture."

"What does this mean?" he asks.

"I don't know." I bend down, kissing Celeste on the

forehead. "You truly are a genius. You found the girl I've been searching for." I show her the image.

"What's special about her?"

"I can't put my finger on it," I answer truthfully. "But I feel like we're on the path to figuring it out."

We spend the rest of the day exploring the other homesites Celeste added to Viktor's phone app. Only one of the homes is still standing, or at least halfway standing. The only things remaining are the four walls. While there, she puts one of her Ph.D. degrees to work and finds several classifications of plants that were believed to have been extinct, making her very excited.

"Where do you want me to take you?" Viktor asks on our way back into the city. Today has been just what I needed, even though I didn't realize it at the time. I turn, looking at my tiny maker in the back seat. She's studying a book larger than anything I used in college and scribbling notes in a notebook.

"Home. Take me home."

FIFTEEN

angel of death

TWO DAYS later I receive the phone call I'd been dreading. Roger invited Josh to attend a meeting of "The Silver Bullets," and the meeting is this evening.

"We need to meet with him before he goes," Viktor reminds me when I relay the information to him.

"I told him we'd be there in an hour to brief him and give him the earpiece. He's waiting for us in my room at the dorm."

"You're one step ahead of me." He smiles.

A million sarcastic responses fill my mind, but I decide to behave and keep them inside. An hour later, we step into my room and find Josh asleep on the bed. "Josh," I whisper.

"I'm up!" He jumps out of bed with a startle.

"It's just me. We brought you a few things." Josh looks between me and Viktor. "This is Viktor. He's my...friend."

"Are you a vampire?" Josh asks.

Viktor looks at me before answering. "I am."

Josh sticks his hand out, ready to shake Viktor's. "It's nice to meet you, Viktor."

"It's a pleasure to meet you, too." Viktor pulls the earpiece out of his pocket, handing it to Josh. "This won't be visible to anyone."

Josh slides it into his ear. "What it's for?"

"It allows us to hear you. If you get into trouble or need help, we will come immediately."

"Pick a code word." I pull his hair around in front of his ear, making sure the small piece of plastic is completely invisible.

"A code word?"

"If you need help, you work the word into the conversation. It tells us you need help. You can't use hamburger. It's already taken." I smile remembering the emoji Viktor sent.

"Okay, gosh. Does it have to be food?"

I laugh. "No. It's whatever word you want. Don't make it too hard to work into a sentence, though."

"Spiderman," Josh answers. "My code word is Spiderman."

Viktor slides a similar earpiece into his own ear. "This allows me to hear everything." Josh nods, understanding.

"I'm not sure what to expect," he admits.

I sigh. "It's going to be super awkward and weird. I

felt like I was in the middle of a movie set or something."

"Keep your head down, and don't draw attention to yourself," Viktor adds.

"So, in other words, be me." He takes a deep breath. "I'm going to go downstairs and meet Roger. He thinks I'm at the library, studying. Truthfully, I didn't want to stay in the room with him any more than I had to."

"Where's the meeting?" I ask.

"Oh, sorry. I guess that would help." He pulls out his phone and reads the address to me.

"We'll be right behind you," Viktor reassures him. "If at any time you feel unsafe, don't hesitate to use the code word."

Josh nods, heading toward the door. "Josh?" I call. "Don't tell anyone what you're doing. No matter how much you think you can trust them." He nods and leaves the room.

"What are you thinking?" Viktor asks once Josh is out of earshot.

"I'm thinking he's sweet, innocent, and naive. Their perfect recruit."

"Agreed. Let's go. I don't want something to happen to him." We follow an older model Toyota Camry, with Roger driving, out of the parking lot and toward the Quarter. The parking gods are shining down on us, and we find the perfect parking spot several blocks away from the actual meeting location.

"He's nervous," Viktor says, listening to him mumble. "He didn't say two words on the way here, now he won't stop talking." With only one earpiece, I have to rely on Viktor to keep me up to date with what's going on.

"They're inside. I can hear the chanting. Also, Josh's breathing has sped up."

"Keep calm, Josh," I whisper inspiration as if he can hear me.

"Sounds like they sat down." I picture the meeting I attended and Greg sitting at the front of the room with a mouth full of rotting teeth and a soul full of hate.

"What are they doing?" I whisper. Why am I whispering?

"Still chanting hate while Greg eggs it on. I haven't heard anything about vampires or lycan. Just a lot of hate speech."

"Sounds about right."

"They've stopped chanting. Greg just said something about the bombing and the miracle that was achieved through Zoe's sacrifice."

"What miracle? The only people killed were innocent humans. None of the vampires he..." Viktor waves a hand, hushing me.

"He just told them the bombing was only a drop in the bucket for what they have planned." I feel my eyes open wider. "He asked for new angels."

"Shit," I whisper. "That bastard."

Viktor turns toward me. "Someone close to Josh just volunteered." He covers his ear, listening intently. "Greg is standing very close to the microphone. He just asked who Roger's guest was."

The delay in communication is killing me.

"He introduced Josh as his roommate and friend. I think Greg just hugged Josh. His earpiece made a strange sound."

"Is he okay?" I ask.

Viktor nods. "They're talking. Greg knows Roger, which means he's been to a meeting before."

I should've killed Greg when I had the chance. "Do we need to go in?"

"No. Greg is pairing them into their groups to send them out for research. He separated Roger and Josh." I don't know if that's a good thing or a bad thing. "They're leaving."

"Do we follow them or stop him?"

"We follow. If we blow his cover, we're out of options."

"Do you think Josh will think to send us street names? I forgot to mention that to him."

"He just said, Bourbon. He's still breathing hard."

"Good, boy, Josh." If I were still human, I'd be sweating balls right now.

Viktor pulls the car away from the curb, honking at unsuspecting humans that need to move the hell out of the way. Several streets are still blocked because of the explosion, making it more difficult to navigate than usual. "Dauphine, heading toward Rampart."

"Rampart? That's almost out of the Quarter. Are there any bars up that far?"

"I would imagine so. The Quarter is full of them. He just read the address out loud. Seventeen-forty-six."

I search for information on the address on my phone. "It's a restaurant."

"Are you sure?"

"According to Google, yes. *The Golden Bucket* is the name of it. They specialize in ice cream, chicken fingers, and pizza."

"Can you tell who owns it?" I search their website, unable to find any other information.

"No. Are you thinking it's lycan owned?"

"That's exactly what I'm thinking." He pulls into a parking spot along the street a block away. "They're sitting down."

"Anything happening?"

"Nothing."

I unstrap the seatbelt. "I'm going in."

"Amelia, that's not smart. They know what you look like."

"We don't know who's with him," I retort. "It could be someone who doesn't know me from Adam."

Viktor holds up a hand. "Wait. Josh is talking to someone."

The lag in communication is going to be the death of me! He turns toward me. "Edon's in there."

Oh, my God. "Is Edon their target?"

"I don't think so. Greg told them to scout and research tonight. I assume that means no killing."

"Viktor, does Edon own this restaurant?"

He pulls out his phone and sends a text. Moments later it buzzes. "He doesn't own it, but it is lycan owned."

"Shit," I whisper. "We have to warn Edon."

"Done." He lowers his phone, covering his ear with his palm. "Edon just asked the group to leave."

"Are they doing it?"

"Not willingly. Josh isn't saying much, so I'm not sure what's going on."

I picture him wide-eyed and scared. "God, I feel so guilty for sending him into this."

"They're going to a second location," Viktor says, pulling away from our spot. "He just said Conti Street." We drive the short distance to Conti, finding a spot to park, and I catch a glimpse of Josh's group. Five lost souls follow an older man toward an unmarked door.

"There they are." I point out the front window.

"Stay here, Amelia," Viktor warns again. "At this point, you'll only get in the way." I sigh, knowing he's right, but shit, he's pissing me off.

"Then you need to give me play-by-play transcripts of what's going on." I cross my arms in front of my chest, trying to ease the frustration.

"Someone greeted them at the door. An older man asked for the answer to a riddle, and someone answered. It sounds like they're sitting down." Viktor covers his ear again. "Josh just asked why all of the curtains are torn to shreds, and no one really answered him."

It suddenly dawns on me, that I covered the fact that vampires are real, but never covered lycan with him. He's either going to get the shock of his life or scream his code word if this is a wolf bar.

"One of the group members is spewing hate about the lycan."

"What's Josh saying? I forgot to tell him they're real."

Viktor turns to me. "I don't think it's a wolf bar. Someone is doing poetry."

"Is it Opie?" I ask. "If so, he's about to discover witches are real. He's going to be traumatized when this is over."

"They're about to leave. The older man in the group just directed the group out, saying something about returning their finds to Greg." Viktor starts the SUV.

"What finds?"

"I don't know, but this is the way they choose their targets." We manage to park not far from the original meeting spot.

"We need to warn everyone. All of the vampires and lycan. Any of these places could be their next target. I won't sit back and watch more innocent people be injured or worse because of Greg and these lost people."

"I agree. I'll call a meeting tonight," he answers, listening to his earpiece.

"Tonight? Why the hell hasn't a meeting been called before now? Too many people have been allowed to be hurt while you all just sit on your asses watching from afar."

Viktor turns to face me completely. "Not all vampires believe like you and me. To them, this is a human issue and purely a human issue. Most vampires haven't been human for centuries and have forgotten what it's like or don't care anymore. I cannot speak for the lycanthrope, but I imagine many of them feel the same. Remember Drew? He was the one that alerted the vigilante group of the bar's whereabouts."

"He did because he wanted out. How many others feel the same?" I ask.

"Josh is on his way out. He says Roger is gone, and he wants to talk with us." Viktor covers his ear, which has become the universal symbol for "Be quiet, Amelia." "He wants us to meet him at the cathedral."

Pedestrian traffic has picked up, making it take longer to get three blocks in a car than it should. The parking gods must shine down on Viktor because, yet again, he manages to find a spot alongside the cathedral. Minutes later, Josh slides into the backseat.

I turn, facing my friend. "Are you okay?" I expect to see a traumatized kid in freak-out mode. Instead, he's smiling, ear to ear.

"Are you kidding? I'm more than okay! It was like being in the middle of a spy movie, and I was the spy. Here." He hands me a small notebook. "I took notes." I open the spiral-bound book to find words scribbled all over the first few pages.

"You weren't scared?"

"Maybe at first, but then I remembered that I'm an undercover spy and did my job." He laughs loudly. "That was the most fun I've ever had!" He slides forward in the seat, putting his head between mine and Viktor's. "Why did no one tell me that werewolves are real? Oh, my God." He slides back, clapping his hands. "This is amazing!"

"What happened to Roger?"

"Hmm? Oh, I don't know. He disappeared after he volunteered for some angel thing."

Viktor looks in the rearview mirror. "He's the one that volunteered to be the angel?"

"He did. I don't know what that means, but Greg got excited when Roger volunteered. Speaking of Greg, I'm not sure what to think about him."

"He's a psychopath," I answer. "We're taking you back to the dorm. I don't want you to stay in your room. Use mine, I won't be there."

"Okay, why?"

"If Roger's agreed to be the angel, you need to stay as far away from him as possible."

"What does that even mean?" he asks.

"It means he's the next to die."

Josh slides back in his seat. The look of pure joy he had moments earlier is replaced with sadness. "Are you sure that's what it means?"

"More than likely," Viktor answers for me.

"How can we stop him?"

"We're working on that now," Viktor says. "Josh, we may need you to go back in for more information. Are you willing to do that?"

"Yes," he whispers. "If it'll save my friend." Viktor stops in front of the dorm, and Josh exits, much less excited than before. "Let me know what I need to do."

We watch as he enters the common room and disappears up the stairs.

"I don't like using him."

"Yeah, me either, but he did well," Viktor adds.

"Are we going home for the meeting?"

"No. I won't bring that group into the same building as Celeste. Meetings are held in the Quarter, in the LaLaurie mansion." I turn toward Viktor, not sure I understood correctly.

"The LaLaurie mansion? Are you shitting me?"

"I bought the house after we...*took care* of Madame LaLaurie." He speaks about one of the most important terrifying historical facts in the city of New Orleans like it's an everyday occurrence.

"The stories about her are true?"

He sighs. "They were. We took care of her."

An image of vampires "taking care" of a situation flashes to mind. "How do we get in touch with them and let them know about the meeting?"

Viktor smiles. "Already done. I texted them earlier."

meeting at a haunted mansion

WE PARK in front of the abandoned mansion I've walked past hundreds of times. The story that accompanies the building is one of horror, and even when I didn't believe in the paranormal, I avoided this place like the plague. Tourists stop, taking pictures of the beautiful, haunted building, and move quickly past.

"Do we have to go inside?"

"That's generally where the meetings are held," he answers with a smirk.

"Inside, really? Why don't you wear the earpiece, and I'll listen in from out here."

Viktor laughs, opening my door for me. "Aren't you the brave one? Come on, I'll introduce you to the Madame. She still hangs around from time to time."

"Okay, so I was getting out until you said that. Now, I'm sitting my butt right here."

"Come on, mon amour. The hype that surrounds

this house is much more than the actual house itself." He laces his fingers through mine, leading me to the front door of the mansion. "They should begin arriving soon."

Viktor enters a code into a numbered box hidden behind a false shutter. "That's ingenious," I whisper, following him inside the ancient home. The smell of must and old house hits me instantly.

"Are you open for tours?" I turn to see a large woman standing in the door frame with a camera strapped around her neck.

"No, ma'am." I move to close the door.

"Oh, come on. We won't bother anything." She begins ushering her family through the door. "We just love old houses, especially haunted ones. My kids love watching those ghost shows on cable. Especially the one where the guy yells at the ghosts the entire time."

Viktor moves in front of the woman. "Madame, I'm going to have to ask you to leave immediately." He's using a strong French accent, something I've never heard from him before. "This home is privately owned and operated. Your stepping foot inside the door has surely upset Madame LaLaurie, and we shall hope there are no repercussions."

The woman looks around the room nervously. "Is that possible?"

"Oui," he answers. Just then a loud crash comes from a room behind us.

"Okay, thank you." She mumbles, ushering

everyone back through the door. "I'm so sorry we interrupted. Sorry, Ms. Laurie! You go on haunting, or whatever it is you do," she shouts into the house.

Viktor locks the door behind the family and turns with a smirk. "That was fun."

"Looks like I came at the right time," a man walks out of the room where the noise came from. He's tall and thin with a chiseled jawline and curly blonde hair.

"Phillipe!" Viktor says, rushing toward the man and shaking his hand. "Yes, your timing was impeccable." Phillipe turns toward me. "Who is this lovely specimen?"

"Amelia," I answer as he takes my hand into his, kissing the top gently. Green eyes linger on mine longer than necessary, bringing tingles to the places our skin meets.

"Don't hog the fresh blood, Phillipe." Another man enters the room. He's wearing a red tracksuit and doesn't look like anyone's version of a vampire. He's almost the same height as I am, which means he's a little over five feet tall. He's as wide as he is tall, and the red outfit doesn't help disguise his size.

"I do apologize, Brian," Phillipe says, stepping to the side.

"Brian Jones," the short vampire says, shaking my hand.

"Amelia Lockhart," I respond.

Brian smiles. "Where have you been hiding this one, Viktor?"

"Away from you, Brian," a familiar voice says, coming in the front door. I look up to see Violet and Oliver. She rushes to my side, wrapping her arms around me. "How are you holding up?"

"I'm good." I look around the haunted mansion. "I'd prefer to meet somewhere else, however."

"Yeah, this place bothered me at first, too. But in all the times I've been here, I've never seen anything scary." She wraps her arm through mine, leading me to a back room with chairs and a large table. It looks like it should be in a conference room rather than a nine-teenth-century haunted mansion.

"Erick's out of town," Brian announces.

"Where's he gone? He's been away for a few years. Are we sure he's still alive?" Phillipe asks with a smirk.

Brian shrugs his shoulders. "Who knows with that one? He's probably out courting women. Will Chamberlin be joining us?" he asks Violet.

"No, Harrison won't be joining us," Violet adds with a smirk.

Phillipe leans back in his chair. "So, the rumors are true?"

"Aye, they are," Ollie answers. His words almost sound protective, and I can't help but notice how close Violet and Ollie are sitting. I make a mental note to ask for more information later.

"Why are we here?" Phillipe asks Viktor.

"We're waiting on one more guest." On cue, a loud knock sounds on the door. Viktor stands from his seat, disappearing into the front room. He returns seconds later with Edon on his heels.

"Absolutely not," Brian says, standing from his seat. "I will not lower myself to sit at a table with a dog."

"*You* lower yourself? I think you're confused, tiny man." Brian steps in front of Edon, barely coming past his chest. His intimidation tactics are clearly not working.

"I asked Edon to be here tonight to represent the lycan. This involves them, too." Viktor pulls his chair out, sitting next to me. "Sit, gentlemen."

Edon steps away from Brian, sitting on the other side of me. Brian sits in his chair, crossing his arms over his chest. "What is so important that we have to invite dogs to our meeting?"

"I'm not excited to be near you either, bloodsucker," Edon retorts.

"Gentlemen," Viktor interrupts. "I called everyone here because of a group of vigilantes that are targeting both vampires and wolves."

"Have you found more information?" Edon asks.

"We have," Viktor answers.

Brian leans back in his chair. "This is beginning to bore me."

I met this vampire five minutes ago, and I'm already ready to kill him. "Perhaps if you listened, you might not feel the same way." I fling my frustrations at him.

He turns toward me with hatred in his eyes. "How

dare you speak to me like that. Do you know who I am?" Brian stands from his chair.

"No, and I don't care to know. From my perspective you're a little man, suffering from little man syndrome, who needs to learn when to shut up." The vampire is in front of me within seconds, baring his teeth.

"How dare you speak to me with such a tone? Viktor should've taught you better manners." He turns his attention toward Viktor. "Although you don't have the best reputation for choosing women, do you?"

Movement happens so quickly I barely have time to process what happened. Within seconds, Brian is slammed into a wall, and Viktor is standing underneath him, with his hand wrapped around his throat. The short vampire actually looks scared. "Don't ever confuse my complacency with your mouth with your ability to disrespect or threaten those I care about." He lets go, allowing the short vampire to slide down the wall. "You owe Amelia an apology, now."

"I owe no one an apology."

"Brian," Phillipe warns. "Viktor has given you a warning. I suggest you take it as such."

The short red man turns toward me with hatred filling his eyes. "I apologize, Amelia." His words are laced with venom.

"Apology accepted," I mumble. Neither of us means our words. I don't like him, and clearly, the feeling is mutual.

It takes a few moments for the energy in the room

to settle. Edon hasn't said much since sitting but smiles at the spectacle in front of him. "Good job," he whispers in my ear. It seems everyone in this room has a common dislike for Brian, the poorly dressed, annoying vampire.

"Back to the matter at hand. What is so important that it involves both of our communities?" Phillipe brings the room back to the reason we're here.

"We discovered a group of vigilantes, set on destroying the vampire and lycan communities in the Quarter." Viktor looks each member in the eye as he speaks. "They're the ones responsible for the bombing a few nights ago."

"Human vigilantes?" Brian asks. "What does this have to do with us? Humans will be humans."

"It has to do with us because they're being led by an ancient vampire," Viktor answers.

Phillipe slides forward. "How ancient?"

"Older than me." Viktor props his elbows on the table.

"There is no one older than you in the city," Phillipe answers.

"Penelope is," Violet speaks for the first time.

The men look between themselves. "Penelope? Your wife, Penelope?" Brian asks. "No offense." He holds his hands in front of his face. "Isn't she dead?"

"I thought she was. Turns out she's alive and well and living in our city."

"How is that possible? How would we not know?" Phillipe stands. "Hell, how could *you* not know?"

Viktor ignores the question, and Violet takes over. "No one has seen her, but it has to be her."

"I've seen her," I answer. "A year ago. It was definitely her."

"How do you know it was her?" Brian asks.

"Because it was," Viktor answers, clearly done with Brian and his questions. "She's the one backing the vigilante group. Although, they don't know it."

"Why? It makes no sense. She's stronger than all of us. If she wanted us dead, she could easily perform the task herself." Phillipe asks the million-dollar question.

"Because in her mind, this is a game, and we're all pawns on her board to control and manipulate. She's got all the time in the world. She's not in a hurry, nor does she care who or how many she hurts along the way." Viktor's words sound sad as he speaks.

"With intentions of killing all of us, she's planning on killing countless humans and lycan," Oliver speaks for the first time. "This has been going on in other states, and now it has arrived here in New Orleans. No matter what you believe of humans or wolves, we cannot allow this to happen."

"If it's been going on in other states, let it be their problem. Why does it fall upon us to stop her?" Brian asks.

"Because those attacks were leading up to this." Viktor leans back in his chair.

"How do we stop her?" Phillipe copies Viktor's movement.

"That's what we figure out together," Viktor answers. "We have a human that has agreed to infiltrate the cult."

"Then it's simple. We strap a bomb on this human and send them into a meeting. Problem solved," Brian answers with a smile. I glare at the tiny man across the table, willing him to die.

"That is not a solution," Phillipe answers. "We can't kill more to prevent deaths."

"We have to stop Penelope," I add. "With her gone, the group will disband from lack of leadership. She's using them in the first place. Their cult leader is a nobody with no leadership skills. He's just another one of Penelope's puppets that she has the ability to manipulate."

Brian sits back in his chair. "And how do you propose we do that, young lady? None of us are strong enough to defeat her."

"Alone, no. Together, yes."

"She has a weakness," Viktor says softly.

"Are you going to share what that weakness is?" Brian asks.

Viktor turns toward me. His eyes are full of worry. He takes a deep breath. "No."

Brian slams his short arms on the table. "Then it looks like this meeting was a complete waste of time, and I'm leaving." He slides his chair under the table.

"Penelope has left me alone, and as far as I'm concerned, I will return the favor. I bid you farewell." He nods, stepping away from the table and out the back door.

Phillipe stands, ready to leave when Viktor stops him. "Wait." Phillipe turns back. "This stays in this room." Phillipe sits back in his chair. "Everyone in this room knows her weakness except for you two." He nods toward Phillipe and Oliver, who share a confused look.

Viktor takes another breath. "When Penelope and I were human and married, we had a daughter, Celeste. She's immortal and still alive."

Phillipe stands quickly from his seat. "An immortal child? That's...that's blasphemy."

"No, she's perfect," I interrupt. Viktor places his hand on top of mine.

"She's her weakness."

"Are you suggesting we use the child to lure and kill her?" Oliver asks.

"That's precisely what I'm suggesting," Viktor answers.

A knot forms in my stomach, thinking about using Celeste as bait. So many things could go wrong. I refuse to let anything happen to her.

"I need to meet the child," Phillipe demands.

"No, you do not," Viktor rebukes. "She is under my protection and should anything happen to her, it will result in complete destruction and death. Do I make myself clear?"

Phillipe bows his head. "Perfectly." Anger pours from Viktor.

"At no time will the child be put in danger."

Oliver and Phillipe nod in understanding. I wouldn't dare undermine his authority, but my heart is screaming at the possibility of putting Celeste in danger. I know Viktor will protect her with his life, but that doesn't make it any easier.

"That went well," Violet says once Phillipe has left.

"Viktor?" He puts a hand up, stopping my words.

"I know, and I won't. She's not going to be put in any danger." He laces his fingers through mine, bringing our joined hands to his lips and kissing the back of mine. "I promise."

SEVENTEEN

penelope chambers

THE CAR RIDE back to Mandeville is quiet. I'm still pissed at him for even mentioning Celeste, let alone using her as bait for Penelope. How could he put her in danger like this?

"I know what you're thinking," he announces, nearly halfway across the lake.

"Do you, Viktor?"

He sighs. "You're angry because you think I'm endangering Celeste's life."

"That's exactly what you've done, and yes, I'm pissed. How could you do that to her?"

"If you think for one moment that I would put my child's life at risk, then you don't know me at all. Celeste is my life. I would die for her."

I turn toward him, tears streaming down my cheeks. "Then why? They know about her. What if one of them gets angry at you and tells someone higher up? What if they kill her?"

"She is stronger than any of them, for one thing. Celeste fought Harrison, her maker, and nearly won. She's stronger than any of those bastards there tonight. She's not helpless. I've taught her everything I know and then some. I would choose her in a fight over Oliver or Phillipe any day." I swear he wipes a tear from his cheek. "Trust me when I say, I would never put her life in danger. But she's the key to stopping Penelope."

"How do you know? Penelope left her. Left her own child and pretended to be kidnapped and dead. She loves herself more than she loves you or your child." I instantly regret my words.

Viktor is quiet. "I know," he whispers. "Believe me, I know."

"I'm sorry. That wasn't fair."

"No, you're right. I...we clearly weren't enough for her." Moments later, we pull into the garage of the Mandeville house. Celeste is at the car door before I get the tear stains wiped from my cheeks.

"What's wrong?" she asks, wiping my cheek with her tiny hand.

"Nothing," I lie. I smile, pretending to be happy.

"Oh, for goodness sake. I may look like a child, but I'm not. What happened? Daddy, what did you do?"

I laugh at her question. "I think it's time we have a conversation," Viktor says.

"Okay. You're acting weird." She holds my hand,

leading me inside the house. "What's going on?" Celeste climbs into my lap when I sit down, wrapping her arms around my neck.

"How was your day?" I ask, changing the subject.

"Boring. I did trigonometry all day. Don't try to change the subject."

Viktor walks back into the room with Fran right behind. "We need to talk." He takes a deep breath. "Penelope's still alive, and she's in New Orleans."

"I know. Amelia already told us, remember?"

"I do," he answers. "But it's not that simple. She's trying to hurt other people. She's trying to hurt me and Amelia."

Celeste jumps off my lap. "What? Why would she do that?"

"Because she's not the mother you remember," he offers.

"Does...does she want to hurt me?" Her words are barely a whisper.

"No, sweetheart. She loves you."

"But she wants to hurt you and Amelia?" Viktor nods. "Why?"

"Because she wants control of the city. She wants control of everything."

"How would hurting you or Amelia help her gain control?" I stare at the tiny vampire in awe. She's able to reason better than Brian.

"It's not just us she's after. She wants to hurt the lycan, too."

Celeste sits on a chair across the room. "I'm sorry, Amelia."

I scrunch my forehead. "You're sorry? Why?"

"I'm sorry for what my mother is doing."

"Oh, sweet girl. It's not anyone's fault but her own. You don't owe me an apology for something you have no control over." My eyes fill with tears. "Do you know how strong you are?" She shakes her head. "You are brilliant, kind, loving, and the best person I've ever known."

Celeste runs back to my side, jumping in my lap. "I love you, Amelia."

"I love you, too, Celeste. I'm not going to let anything happen to you."

She pulls away, moving to her father's lap. "Daddy, I love you, too."

He wraps his arms around her tiny body, pulling her close. "Amelia's right. You're the best out of all of us."

"Then you have to trust me when I say I know how to stop her."

Viktor pulls back. "How?"

"Use me. She's my mother, maybe there's something left inside of her that will remember that. When she comes to get me, you kill her."

"I don't know if I can," Viktor whispers.

"You can, and you will." She jumps off his lap and claps her hands together. "It's time for a plan." She sticks her hand in the air. "Oh, Amelia. I found something for you." She runs upstairs, coming back seconds later with a stack of papers.

"What are these?"

"Information I found on the Chambers Plantation. I printed off all of the pictures and information available on the internet. There were a few more photographs of the little girl you found." I flip through the papers, seeing the image of the young girl. "It's weird though." She pulls three papers from the stack. "This picture was from 1862." She picks up another one and shows it to me. "This one is from 1872." The girl is in both pictures and looks the same age in both.

"Is that the same girl?"

"I think so." She turns both pictures over, showing the initials O.M.C. for her picture.

"That's the same thing written underneath the one I found."

Celeste stacks the papers back into neat rows. "One mystery at a time. Let's figure out how to stop Penelope, and then we'll figure out who this ghostly child is."

"Yes, Mom," I answer, kissing her forehead.

"How are we going to do this?" she asks her father.

Viktor takes a deep breath. "We get word to Penelope that you're still alive."

"Okay, how are we going to do that?"

"Through Greg," I answer. "I'm guessing she's in contact with him regularly."

"I don't know who this Greg person is, but okay," Celeste adds. "And then what?"

"God, you're pushy," Viktor says with a laugh.

"I'm thorough. You've always taught me to have a plan and a backup plan. I'm just doing what I was taught."

"She's got you there." I laugh.

Viktor sighs. "We lure her to a location, thinking you will be there, and then I take care of the situation."

"Daddy, you just said you didn't know if you could kill her. How is this a good plan?"

"Because I'm the only one strong enough."

"We could contain her," I say, making them both turn and stare.

"How could we do that?" Celeste asks.

"I read about it in one of the books in your library. It was only a paragraph or two, but I remember reading how an ancient vampire was trapped in a pit in Romania for over a thousand years. He was kept alive by throwing a goat into the pit once a month."

"That sounds horrible," Celeste whispers.

"Do you think you could find that passage again?" Viktor asks.

"To be honest, no. I read so many books from both yours and Harrison's libraries, I couldn't place everything I read."

"Let me try." Celeste pulls out a MacBook and starts typing.

"If we could trap her, is that crueler than killing

her?" Viktor asks. "What would be the purpose of keeping her alive? Torture? Cruelty? There's no kindness in that."

"There's no kindness in killing every vampire and lycan in the city so she can take over either," Celeste spews from behind her keyboard.

"What do you remember about her?" Viktor asks his daughter. "I never knew her as a vampire. Was she... was she cruel?"

Celeste stops typing. "She ignored me for him. She stopped being my mother and left me to fend for myself."

"She ignored you for Harrison?"

She nods. "She acted like she was happy."

Viktor's face changes immediately. "Excuse me," he whispers, standing from his chair. "I'm going to go clean up a little. We'll work on the plan a little later."

"I'm sorry, Daddy."

"No, don't be." He kisses the top of her head before heading upstairs. Celeste watches until he's out of sight.

"I upset him."

"No, sweetheart. It's not you. It's Penelope." I move closer to her side. "Have you found anything?"

"On the vampire in the pit, no. But I did find something you might be interested in." She pulls up a photograph from the Chambers Plantation. "Look at this."

I pull the screen closer, trying to decide what I'm looking at. "What is this?"

"It's a picture of Mrs. Chambers, Harrison's wife. Look at the hair."

"It's a black-and-white photo, and she's facing backward. What am I supposed to see?"

She opens a program on her computer and works photo magic on the old photograph, somehow making it clearer and in color. "Ta-da!"

The woman on the screen has long curly red hair. "You don't think...?"

"That this is a picture of Penelope?" she interrupts. "Who else would it be?"

"Holy shit." My eyes open wide. "Oh, Celeste, I'm sorry. I didn't mean to curse in front of you. Your dad needs to see this."

"I'm not sure now is the best time."

"Harrison told me once that Penelope died in 1829. This photograph is from at least 1870. That bastard lied about everything. The entire time they were together, living as husband and wife, and right under Viktor's nose."

Celeste keeps typing, pulling up something that looks like a family tree. "According to this lovely time-line someone added on Ancestry, Penelope Chambers died in 1910, leaving behind two children. Dorothea Rae Chambers and Odilia Mae Chambers."

"O.M.C." I pull the photograph of the young girl from my bag. "That has to be this girl. What happened to the other one?"

"Vampires can't have children," Celeste states the obvious.

I grab the pile of papers she handed me earlier. "These aren't ordinary children."

"Maybe Daddy was right, and they're immortal children, like me?" she asks, almost hopeful.

"I don't think so. Look at her eyes." The girl looks sad, solemn, and unhealthy. "If she were a vampire, she'd look healthy."

"It would explain why she's the same age in every photograph."

"True. But there has to be another explanation." I put all of the photographs, side by side, comparing them to one another. The background changes in each, but the girl looks the same.

A loud knock on the door, makes both of us jump. "It's a vampire," Celeste whispers.

"Do you recognize them?" She shakes her head. "Go get Viktor." She moves at vampire speed up the stairs, making the papers strewn across the floor fly.

The two of them return seconds later. "Who is it?" Viktor asks through the door.

"Phillipe," a familiar voice answers.

"Why are you here, Phillipe? This is my home, not somewhere I choose to meet with others."

"I understand, and I apologize, but I thought you'd want to see this. I'm walking off of the porch and onto the driveway. Come outside if you feel comfortable."

Phillipe's footsteps decrescendo as he does what he says he's going to do.

"Celeste?" Viktor warns.

"I know, basement."

Viktor nods, heading out of the back of the house, to meet Phillipe.

"Come on," Celeste pulls my hand, and we head toward the familiar basement. The same basement where Harrison nearly killed me, and Celeste turned me into a vampire. We're in the basement no longer than a few minutes when Celeste announces Viktor called us to come out.

"How do you know? I didn't hear anything."

"Remember, Daddy and I can communicate. He says to come out, that we're safe." I follow her back to the living room and find Phillipe sitting on the couch across from Viktor.

He stands as we enter. "Phillipe, may I present Celeste Marie Luquire, my daughter."

Phillipe bows at the hip. "C'est un plaisir de vous rencontrer, jeune."

Celeste curtsies. "It's a pleasure to meet you, as well."

"Phillipe brought this photograph with him." Viktor hands me a picture. "It was taken a few hours ago." In the picture stand three people. Penelope, Greg, and Roger."

"Where was this taken, and how did you get it?"

"It was on the Riverwalk, and one of my...associates took it."

"Roger is supposed to be their next angel."

"What does that mean?" Phillipe asks.

"It means he's going to kill whomever they send him after in hopes of becoming an angel of death," I answer.

"What kind of screwed-up mess is that?" He looks between the three of us.

"It's Penelope," Viktor answers.

Phillipe stands. "I apologize for coming to your home. After our meeting earlier, I felt like this was something that couldn't wait."

"Agreed. Thank you for bringing it to my attention." The two men shake hands.

Once Phillipe has gone and Celeste is convinced he's out of earshot, she pulls up the image and information we discovered. "What's this?" Viktor asks.

"It's Harrison Chambers' wife."

"Is that Penelope?" He stares at the woman who's turned around in the photo.

Celeste and I share a look. "We think so," she answers.

"I'm ready for this to be over with." His voice sounds sad.

"As long as she lives, she will find a way to destroy you," Celeste says softly. "She has to die."

"I know, mon petit amour. I know."

EIGHTEEN

erick

THE NEXT MORNING, I head toward Tulane and my dorm to check in with Josh. Celeste wasn't overly excited at letting me out of her sight, but I promised we'd go over the information on Chambers Plantation when I got back, and she relented.

Opening the door to my floor, I run into Samantha. She looks past me, no doubt looking for my "uncle."

"He's not with me," I disappoint her.

"Oh, okay." She smiles a fake smile. "Are you just getting back? I could have sworn I heard you in your room this morning. It sounded like you fell out of bed, breaking a few things on the way down." She laughs.

"Yeah, I knocked over a vase before I left for breakfast." My inner alarm bells start ringing.

"There's a broom and mop in the hall closet if you need it. Have a great day."

"You too, Sam."

I wait until she leaves the floor before knocking on the door. "Josh," I whisper. "Josh," I try again. The door is unlocked when I turn the knob. Shit. "Josh?" The room is empty and just like Samantha suggested, a shattered vase, along with everything else breakable is thrown across the floor.

> Josh is gone, and the room is destroyed.

> On my way

Sliding my phone back into my pocket, I make my way around the room, looking for some sort of clue as to what happened. A blood stain on the floor is the first thing I notice. I can smell that it belongs to Josh. "What happened, Josh?" I whisper, looking around the room for more clues.

My phone buzzes.

> If you want to see your friend again, meet at the Riverwalk.

> Who is this?

> A mutual friend.

> How do I know you're telling me the truth?

Moments later a photograph pops on the screen. It's Josh, and he's wearing a blindfold, and his hands are bound.

> Come alone, or he dies.

> Not a very original line.

> Fifteen minutes.

I don't hesitate or inform Viktor, which I have no doubt I'm going to regret later. Ten minutes later, I pull my SUV into a parking spot near the Riverwalk. I don't know which end of the mile-long walk to start on, so I start in the middle.

Crowds of humans steer clear as they pass, some staring, some smiling, but most giving me a wide berth as they pass. For the first time since being changed, I think like a vampire. Using my nose, I sniff the air, searching for a familiar scent. It doesn't take long to locate him. I recognize another odor close to him, Greg. I send a quick text to Viktor.

> At Riverwalk. Greg has him. Following scent.

My phone buzzes immediately.

> Don't move! I'll be there in ten minutes.

> Ten minutes is too late.

I slide the phone back into my pocket, ignoring the constant vibrations. There's someone else with them. I don't recognize the smell. The further I go, the stronger the recognition becomes. I don't see them, but I know they're nearby. I stop, scanning the area, looking for anything or anyone familiar. A flash of red grabs my attention. Standing near the river is a woman with bright red hair, my red hair, and she's looking right at me.

Without caring who sees me, I move at vampire speed off the walk and straight to her side. "Where is he?"

"Is that any way to greet someone?"

"I don't care how I greet you, bitch. Where's Josh?"

Penelope steps backward. "Let's try this again, shall we?" She holds her hand in front of me. "I'm afraid we haven't been properly introduced. I'm Penelope Luquire-Chamberlin." She smiles.

I take a moment to take in every feature of the thousand-year-old vampire. She's wearing a black pantsuit, complete with overpriced heels. If I didn't know better, I'd think she was a businesswoman in town for a convention. I ignore her hand, leaving it hanging in front of me. "We've met."

She clears her throat and lowers her hand. "Seems Viktor's standards have lowered."

"Where's Josh?" I repeat.

"I'm right here." Josh comes seemingly out of nowhere and moves to Penelope's side. He wraps an arm around her waist, pulling her tight. "Thank you so much for coming to my rescue." His voice returns to the scared, awkward boy from school.

"Josh? What's going on?"

"What's the matter? Is poor little Amelia confused?" Penelope pulls his wrist to her face, biting into his skin and drinking his blood in front of anyone walking by. Josh's face contorts to someone in complete ecstasy. His face changes again to the image of the creature that attacked me a year ago, and Penelope pulls away. "I see the recognition on your face. Yes, Josh is my donneuse and strigoi."

"Josh," I whisper. "Is this true?"

"Do you know how hard it was to listen to you whine? Oh, my God!" His face turns normal again.

"You're wondering how dear sweet Viktor didn't pick up on him, aren't you?"

"No," I lie.

"He's not so all-powerful as he thinks." The laugh that escapes her, makes me want to commit murder. "That's what drinking animal blood will do for you. Of course, he was always weak. It's the reason I left him."

"Harrison took you."

Her laugh reminds me of a serial killer. "God, does he still believe that after all these years? What a bore."

She nods toward me. "Take her." A cloth covers my head from behind, and something metallic wraps around my wrists. Pain shoots through my arms, bringing me to my knees. I try to scream, but my voice won't work.

Josh laughs. "Does it hurt, widdle baby?" His words are the last I hear before the world goes black.

......

My eyes open to complete darkness. It takes a few moments to come to the realization that I'm hanging upside down with my wrists and ankles bound. A gag prevents me from screaming as I flail back and forth, trying to break my bonds. *Stop and think, Amelia.* I work at slowing my breathing, focusing on what I know from the room. I can't see anything, even with vampire vision, which most likely means I'm in some sort of deprivation room. The smell of rotting flesh is nearly overwhelming, and the sound of a constant, steady drip is the only sound I hear. Dammit, Amelia. You knew better than this!

"Hello!" I scream, my words sounding more like a mumble than words. "Help!" My voice echoes through the room. Where the hell am I?

A door cracks open, flooding the room with light. Against the walls are the remains of bodies. Each one is in different stages of decomposition. The few closest to the door are missing body parts. Oh, my God. "Yeah, you're awake!" Penelope claps her hands as she walks in. "What do you think of your room? I hope it was to your liking?" I scream, but nothing comes out. "I know. The view isn't the best, but you'll get used to it." She turns away from my swinging body. "Josh sends his regards." She closes the door, leaving me alone with the decomposing humans and returns me to the dark.

Being immortal means she can keep me tied like this for eternity. I kick my legs, trying to free myself without any luck. "It's no use," a voice whispers from behind. "You're not going to get loose." I try turning my body toward the voice without luck. Whoever it is, coughs, followed by a sickening sound of liquid hitting something solid. "Hell, I think she's forgotten I'm even in here. The fabric around your mouth will eventually break down and fall off. Then you'll be able to speak."

So, in a hundred years or so, I'll be good. I scream, my frustration sounding through the binding. I can't stay here that long.

"She's a bitch, you know," the voice says. "I'm grateful to have someone to talk to. The last guy didn't make it long. Of course, he was human. They only last a few months or so. Unless she hangs them upside down, then they only last a few hours to days." How is this man talking about this like it's normal? "What did you do to piss her off?" He laughs. "Oh, I forgot you can't answer." His laugh turns into a cough, followed by the wet sound again. "Have you ever been so hungry that you forget you're hungry? That's where I am. I haven't eaten in God knows how long, and these rotting corpses around me aren't even piquing my interest." I hear a chain rattling behind me. "Forgive me for not introducing myself. My name is Erick. We'll have to shake hands later."

Erick? I remember that name. He was the vampire that Brian announced was out of town at the meeting at LaLaurie mansion. Dammit, Brian must be working with Penelope. Viktor was right. I grunt, trying to let the vampire know I recognize his name.

"You smell familiar," he announces. "You smell like Luquire." I make as much noise as possible. "He's your maker?" Erick asks. "I thought he was out of the maker business." He laughs. "Seems he's been keeping a little secret."

He sniffs the air again. "You also smell like Chamberlin." Seriously? It's been a year. Do I still smell like that asshole? "He was never my favorite. Don't tell him that." Erick laughs again. "Who am I kidding? I'm never getting out of this hellhole. Neither are you. Penelope is older and stronger than me. I got a little too close to discovering who she was. It's how I managed to land myself here. I'm guessing the same happened to you." I grunt one time.

"I have an idea," Erick says through a cough. "I'll ask you a question, and you grunt once for yes and twice for no," I grunt once. "Okay, let's do this."

"Is Viktor your maker?" Two grunts.

"Hmm, okay. Do you know him?" One grunt.

"Did you know he and Penelope used to be married?" One grunt.

"Is that what this is about? Is she jealous of you because of him?" Two grunts.

He laughs. "This is the most fun I've had in a while. Are you new?" One grunt.

"I'm out of questions," he admits. "That was fun while it lasted." A hint of a British accent sounds through his words. I grunt twice.

"Okay. More questions?" One grunt.

"Hmm. Are you hungry?" Two grunts. The sound of a chain dragging across the floor moves closer. "Am I moving closer?" One grunt.

The chain moves closer. "Can you swing toward me?" I don't grunt, just start swinging. It takes a while to gain enough momentum to move further than a few inches. "I'm out of chain length. If you can swing toward me, I can catch you and get that gag out of your mouth or free your arms."

His words build hope in my soul. I swing harder and harder until I feel the wind from something swinging toward me. "I almost had you, I think. Grunt when you're coming toward me."

I do as he suggests, making a loud grunt as I approach the area he's in. Weak hands grab at my arms but are not strong enough to hold me tight. Three swings later, I feel his hand hook around my elbow.

"I've got you!" His other arm pulls at the gag

around my mouth, loosening it until it slides to my forehead.

"Oh, thank God!"

Erick laughs. "We did it! Now, let me see what's around your wrists." His arms slide up each arm, working their way to my wrists until he feels the bindings.

"That's it. Can you loosen them?"

He groans as he works at the ties. "I think I've nearly gotten it. The fact that your wrists are bound with nothing more than a small rope goes to show she has clearly forgotten about my existence."

Several minutes later I feel the bindings becoming looser. "They're loose." I pull my wrist, stretching them out even further. I feel it the instant they break. "You did it!" I bend forward, reach the ties around my ankles, and begin working on the binding. I pull the metal braces off of my ankles and drop to the floor with a thud of wetness. I don't want to think about what I landed in.

Erick laughs. "Good job, girl! Get me loose, and we'll get out of here."

I move toward his voice and smell. God, he needs a shower. His arms are outstretched and free, but large chains bind his feet to the wall behind him. Pulling at the chains, I'm able to free him in an instant. The chains have weakened with age.

Erick wraps his arms around me, pulling me close to his emaciated body. "Thank you, love. Now what?"

I pull away from his embrace. "We get the hell out of here."

"It's a plan," he says, wrapping his hand around my elbow. "There's only one problem. I don't know where the door is."

NINETEEN

a new captive

"HOW OFTEN DOES Penelope come into the room?" I ask the exhausted vampire.

"Including today, once." He laughs. "Someone else has deposited the humans. I couldn't tell who they were but could tell they weren't a vampire."

"Then it's up to us to get out of here." His hand is still wrapped around my elbow as we work our way toward the opposite side of the room. "I'm going to search for a doorknob or something that will open the door."

"I mean no disrespect, but do you really think she'd leave the door unlocked?"

I laugh at his question. "As arrogant as she is, I'm surprised she didn't leave it open. Come on, help me find it." We shuffle our way across the floor. Along the way, my feet bump into small pieces of things that feel damp and disgusting. I try not to think about what they most likely are. My nose bumps into the wall, letting me know we've reached our destination.

"Shh," he whispers. "The last thing we want is for someone to hear us."

I begin leading him around the perimeter, trying to decipher what I'm touching. The slick walls are damp and feel metallic. Where the hell are we? My fingers run across what feels like rivets, drilled into the side of the prison walls. Thankfully, I don't touch any of the decomposing bodies I briefly saw.

"Anything?" Erick asks.

"Nothing that feels like a door. The room feels like a circle."

"Like a cylinder?"

"Yes, and made of metal." We walk the circle at least twice, not feeling anything that resembles a door. "I have an idea. Stay here. I'm going to walk around and count how many steps it takes me to return to you."

I leave him attached to the wall and work my way around the circle yet again. Two hundred steps later, I'm behind Erick. "Well, that was effective," he says, pissing me off.

"We can't stay in here until we rot away."

"We can," he answers, pissing me off even more.

"You're a joy, Erick."

"I try," he answers with a chuckle. "Are you wearing shoes?"

"Yes. What does that matter?"

"You need to kick the side of this metal container as

hard as you can. I don't have much strength left, so it's up to you."

"Erick, you said we didn't want anyone to hear us."

"Well, I've changed my mind. You're our only chance out of here. I have nothing left inside me to fight, but you do."

"I won't be able to fight her," I whisper.

"You won't have to. She's going to think you're still tied to the ceiling. As soon as the door opens, you run."

"What about you?"

"I have one foot in the grave anyway." He laughs at his own bad joke, ending in a cough. "Get it? Because I'm a vampire."

"I get it, and I'm not doing it. I won't leave you in here."

Erick laughs again. "I can tell you're young. You still have empathy for others."

"I'll always have empathy for others."

"I believed that once, too." His voice sounds sad. "Kick the wall and stand back."

"I'm not leaving you."

"Just kick the damn wall, young one." I do as he says, kicking with all of my might. The sound echoes through the room. We sit in silence, waiting for someone to rush through the door. Nothing happens. "Try again."

I kick once more, this time adding a scream to the kick. Again, we're met with nothing. "This is no use. Maybe we're alone."

Erick sighs, leaning his weight toward me. "I need to sit down."

"Here," I take his arm, leading him back to the middle of the room.

"Thank you." He pauses. "Did you tell me your name?"

"Amelia. It's nice to meet you, Erick."

"It's very nice meeting you, Amelia. I wish it were under better circumstances."

I sit behind him, giving him something to lean against. "She's going to come back in here for me. There's no way she's going to leave me to die. If that was her plan, she'd have killed me a year ago."

"Let's hope she doesn't wait too long. All this movement has taken a lot out of me." He leans his weight fully onto me and barely weighs anything.

"I'm going to get you out of here, Erick."

It's true vampires don't sleep, but being trapped in this metal prison with no sounds other than Erick's breathing has put me in some sort of hypnotic trance. I've lost track of time and have no idea if it's day or night. Erick hasn't spoken much since our field trip around the room, and I'm worried about him. His breathing has become shallow and ragged.

Viktor's text, telling me to wait for him, plays through my mind on repeat since being locked in here. Why didn't I wait? I'm too damn stubborn for my own good.

Something knocks on the metal from outside.

"Erick?" I whisper.

His mumbles don't form coherent words.

"Did you hear that?" I hear the sound again, this time it's louder. "Okay, I definitely heard something." I move and gently lower Erick to the ground. He's alive but barely conscious.

"Hello!" I scream, not giving a shit if Penelope hears me. The pounding hits again, this time louder. The door creaks open, blinding me with light. Instead of rushing the door, I stand there, like an idiot.

"I see you managed to get down," Penelope says, moving into the room. She covers her nose with her hand. "You might need a shower." Behind her, two men drag in something large. It doesn't take long to realize it's a person with their wrists and ankles bound and a bag over their head. The men throw the person on the ground by the door. "I brought you something to play with." She turns to her helpers. "Uncover his head."

I step back, not sure what's about to happen. When the bag is removed, I gasp at the familiar face. There's a gag in his mouth, and his hair is sticking straight out, but without a doubt, the person on the ground is Viktor. His eyes soften the moment we make eye contact.

"Release him," Penelope orders. The two men step to his sides, releasing his bindings. "Don't even think about it, Viktor," she warns. "You won't win."

Viktor ignores her words and heads straight toward

me, wrapping his arms around me. "Are you okay?" he asks.

I nod, wiping tears. "Erick's not doing well."

"Erick's still alive?" Penelope asks, moving toward the door. "I thought he died years ago." She laughs, closing the door behind her. I stare at every detail, listen to every sound, and notice every crack where the door opened and closed. I don't take my eyes off the location of our means of escape.

"Stay here," I whisper, moving to the same spot she just left. I count the number of rivets through the metal, discovering that there are fewer on this wall. This is the door, and these rivets are the key to finding it again.

"Amelia?" Viktor says, moving toward me. "Where are you?"

"I'm here, and I found the door." I move toward the two men. "Erick, did you hear me? I found the door." Erick moans.

"Why is it so fucking dark in here?" For the first time since I've known him, Viktor uses modern language. "Where are you?"

"I'm coming." I move toward his voice, finding him easily, and wrap my arms around his waist.

"Are you sure you're okay?" he asks, rubbing his hands over my cheeks, checking me for injuries. I nod, covering his hand with mine.

"I'm so sorry I didn't listen to you. You told me to stay, and I..."

"That's water under the bridge. I'm here now."

"Where's Celeste?"

"Safe," is all he says. "I tracked that bitch." He steps back, keeping my hand in his. "I knew she had you."

"How'd you find her?"

"Josh. He may or may not have a broken arm and leg." I don't care if his entire body is broken. That asshole was helping Penelope the entire time.

"You should've broken more than that."

"I'm not done with him. Erick's been missing for years. Looks like you found him." Erick grunts behind us.

"He helped me get loose. I don't know how much longer he's got."

"We need to get all of us out of here." He moves toward Erick. "Can you walk, brother?"

Erick grunts but doesn't move. "I don't think he can. We can't leave him."

"I have no intentions of leaving him. Help me get him up." We move to each side, wrapping our arms around him, and lifting his body weight between us. Erick doesn't try to move his feet as we drag him across the room, and I feel for the rivets that surround the door.

"This is it." Viktor kicks the door full force, making the entire metal container vibrate. The edges of the door crack enough to allow glimpses of outside light to stream in.

"Kick together," he orders. With one arm holding Erick, we kick in unison, knocking the door off its hinges. Daylight floods the room, blinding both of us. "Be prepared for anything or anyone."

Seconds later my eyes adjust to the light, and I stare in shock at our location. "What the hell? Are we on a ship?" Erick grunts a laugh as I look around an empty cargo ship.

"Looks that way." Viktor turns our trio in a complete circle. No land is visible from any angle. "From the looks of it, we're anchored in the Gulf of Mexico a few miles from shore.

"Can you drive it?" I ask, already aware of how dumb of a question it is.

He laughs. "No. There is a way off, though."

"I'm all ears."

Viktor looks at me with a smirk. "We fly."

He's flown several times with me in tow, and I've seen him fly from a distance, but he's confused if he thinks I can fly with him. "*I* can't fly."

"No, but I can. I'll get to the shore and send help. Hell, I'll send the entire Coast Guard if I need to."

"I don't think the Coast Guard is necessary, but a helicopter would be nice." Erick's grunts have changed to moans. Looking at him, I realize his skin is covered in blisters.

"Get him out of the sun," Viktor suggests. "I'll be back as soon as I can."

He leans down and kisses me on the forehead before taking off. I stare in awe as he moves almost faster than my eye can track through the sky. "Shit, I need to learn how to do that."

I pull Erick out of the direct sun, sliding both of us under an overhang. For the first time since meeting him, I see the man who's kept me company for who knows how long. Dark hair is matted close to his skull, and his cheeks and eyes are sunken in, making his face resemble a skeleton more than a human. His skin is caked in dried blood and dirt, and the rags that barely cover his body have more holes than fabric. "It's nice to finally see you, Erick. We're going to get you out of here."

His hand tightens around my arm, letting me know he's still here. I don't know how much time passes before a familiar sound echoes through my ears. "Erick? They're coming." The thumping gets louder as the helicopter approaches. He doesn't move or grunt, but he's still breathing. Moments later a helicopter lands on the back section of the ship. He wasn't lying. Viktor, followed by two soldiers, runs toward us. Viktor reaches us first, wrapping his arms around both of us.

"He's unconscious," I whisper as the soldiers take him from my arm, laying him on a stretcher they pulled from nowhere.

"Don't worry, they're on my payroll." I watch as they search for a vein, trying to get fluid into his body. Instead of clear liquid that would be in a normal IV, this one is full of blood. The moment the fluid enters his body, color begins returning to his skin.

"He's stable," one of the soldiers says. "We need to get him back to the facility."

One of the soldiers turns to me, inspecting me from head to toe. "Ma'am, do you have anything you'd like us to address?"

"No, I'm fine. Take care of him."

"Yes, ma'am." They pick up the stretcher and run toward the helicopter.

Viktor holds my arm. "There's another one coming. Are you sure you don't need to go with Erick?"

"No, I'm fine. Just hungry." He pulls a red bottle from his coat pocket, handing it to me.

I've never been so excited to see goat blood in my life. I finish the bottle in one gulp. "Thank you."

"You're welcome." His hand rests on my cheek as he looks me over for any injuries the soldiers may have missed. "I'm sorry I let this happen," he says, wrapping a blanket around my shoulders.

"You're sorry for letting this happen? I have no one to blame but myself. This was 100 percent my fault. I should've listened to you." I laugh. "I can only imagine what Celeste will have to say about all of this."

"Oh, believe me. She's been filling my ears full. She tried her best to convince me to bring her."

"I'm glad you didn't. I don't know how she would handle seeing Penelope," I admit.

Viktor huffs a laugh. "Probably better than I did."

I pull away, looking into his eyes. "Do you want to talk about it?"

He looks down at our joined hands. "There's not much to say, other than Penelope kindly reminded me of the reasons she deserted both me and our child, faked her death, lived with Harrison, got tired of Harrison, and faked her death again." He laughs. "It wasn't the best conversation I've ever had."

"I'm sorry."

"Me, too." The thumping of helicopter blades interrupts his words.

"Our ride is here." We move side by side to the landing spot, waiting for them to land. Viktor keeps his arm wrapped around my shoulder, and I'm grateful for the connection and his comfort.

We land in the parking lot of what looks like an abandoned building not far out of New Orleans city limits. The number of expensive vehicles and equipment in the parking lot tells me it's anything but abandoned.

"Where are we?"

Viktor looks at the building as we make our way inside. "I don't know how to describe it, except for only a few people are privy to what they do."

"So, secret service type thing."

"Similar." The soldier at the door nods as we approach, no doubt giving us permission to enter.

We enter what looks like a normal hospital emergency room. A woman dressed in scrubs greets us and directs us to a room off of the waiting area. She checks all my vitals and determines that, for a vampire, I'm healthy. "See, I told you." I nudge Viktor's shoulder. "How is the man who was brought in before me?"

"He'll need a day or so to fully recover, but he's going to be okay." She stands, stopping at the door before leaving. "He's stable if you would like to see him."

"Yes, I would. Thank you." She nods, leaving us alone.

I stare at the vampire who once held me captive and now has become my savior. "Did you let Penelope capture you?" Viktor looks up.

"What do you mean?"

"I mean, you're the strongest vampire I know. How did you end up trapped and dropped off with me on an abandoned cargo ship?" He lowers his head. "You did it on purpose didn't you?"

He sits back, running a hand through his messy hair. "Don't be fooled. I'm the strongest vampire *you* know, but Penelope is stronger. She's older and still feeds on human blood. That makes her stronger, no matter her age."

"I'm grateful for you coming to our rescue, but how the hell could you leave Celeste alone? Penelope could've killed you. Why would you take that risk?" I sit up in the hospital bed. "How could you even consider doing that to Celeste? She's lost her mother and then to lose you?" Anger fills me. "Nothing is worth that."

"*You* are worth that." His words are no louder than a whisper.

TWENTY

i really need to
listen better

"IF YOU'D LIKE to visit with Erick, he's awake," the doctor says, coming back into the room. I don't hesitate to follow her.

We walk in to find a middle-aged dark-skinned man, sitting up in bed. "Viktor?" he says with a smile. "What the bloody hell are you doing here?"

"You know me." Viktor smiles. "I have to keep tabs on you at all times."

"Seems you missed a few years," Erick says with a laugh. "Who's this lovely creature you brought with you?"

"Amelia," I answer.

He reaches his hand toward me. "Amelia." My name rolls off of his tongue in a way only a true English accent allows. "My dear, you saved my life."

I move to his bedside, allowing him to take my hand. "You saved my life first. I'd probably still be hanging upside down if it weren't for you." Erick laughs, ending with a cough.

"This would explain why you smelled like Viktor." He looks me up and down. "You look different than I had you pictured."

"Is that a good thing or bad?"

"You are more beautiful than I imagined." He smiles with a mouth full of perfectly white teeth.

"You are just as handsome as I imagined," I retort.

"When you get tired of Luquire, you know where to find me."

Viktor clears his throat. "How did you manage to get yourself locked inside there to start with?"

Erick sighs. "I heard rumors of an ancient vampire in the city. I stuck my nose in where it shouldn't have been and came a little too close to figuring her out."

"Mr. Luquire?" A tall man wearing army fatigues enters the room. "We have some information on the ship. We can talk in the hall."

Viktor looks between the two of us. "Information on the ship pertains to everyone in this room."

"Very well." He pulls a folder from under his arm. "The ship is registered to *Invictus Industries*. They are housed in Slidell and have several cargo ships in the fleet."

"I'm guessing that's a Penelope-owned company," Erick smirks.

The soldier flips through the folder. "The company is owned by a conglomerate from Asia, which led us into a circle of no more information." The man closes the folder and exits.

"In other words, you didn't find anything? That was helpful." Viktor crosses his arms in front of his chest.

"It doesn't matter what the paperwork says, Penelope somehow owns that ship and left us for dead." I sit on the edge of Erick's bed.

"She knew we'd escape," Viktor says from across the room.

"How do you know?"

"Because if she wanted us dead, we'd be dead." He sighs, moving closer to us. "She's playing with us."

"God, I'm so tired of her games. I think Brian's working with her."

"He's been taken care of." He doesn't add any explanation, and I don't ask.

Erick laughs. "Brian is a...what is it the young people say? A wannabe?"

"That's exactly what I thought when I met him." I laugh.

The doctor comes back into the room. "A car is on the way to take you back to the city."

I turn toward Erick. "When will he be able to leave?"

"Mr. Comstock is free to go anytime. His body is recovering quickly." She turns toward Erick. "As fast as you're healing, you should be fully recovered within the next two or three hours."

"Thank you, love. I'm feeling better by the moment.

You saved my life." The doctor blushes before leaving the room.

"Looks like you've gotten your charm back."

Erick wiggles his eyebrows at me. "Never lost it." He's the flirtatious uncle I never knew I needed. The car arrives a few minutes later, and surprisingly, Erick is able to walk without assistance.

Since arriving, I've had three bottles of goat blood, but my body is still craving something. It's like the midnight cravings for chocolate that I remember as a human.

The car stops in front of a brick home in the middle of a suburban subdivision. Erick opens the car door before turning back toward me. "Amelia, I cannot thank you enough for what you did for me back there. I am forever in your debt." He takes my hand into his, rubbing his thumb along the back of my hand, followed by a kiss. "We'll see each other soon."

Chill bumps cover my skin with his words. He was right when he says he never lost his charm. I watch Erick walk into the unsuspecting house and realize, at that moment, he's the vampire books are written about.

Viktor clears his throat. "That was a bit dramatic, don't you think?"

"I kind of liked it."

"I'll remember that." Viktor's words bring a smile to my face.

We sit in silence the rest of the way to Mandeville. I

don't know how much our driver knows about our true identities, but sharing information doesn't seem the smartest. With Erick in the car, the two of us sat close together, making room for all three of us on one seat. With Erick gone, neither of us has moved, and our bodies are in contact from shoulder to ankle. The comfort of his touch helps ease the frustration of Penelope.

The car parks in front of the house, and Viktor freezes in place. "Driver, don't stop."

"What's going on?" I ask, watching the house disappear in the rear window.

He turns toward me. "I need you to trust me right now. This is not a time for one of your hero moments. Do you understand?"

I nod. "You're scaring me. Celeste?"

He shakes his head, and I relax slightly. "The driver is going to take you to one of the homes in the Quarter. Please, do as I ask."

"You're not coming?"

He pulls my hand to his lips, copying Erick's move from earlier, and kisses the back of my hand. "I'll be safe, mon amour. Promise me you will, too."

"I promise. I'll stay put." I have no intentions of doing anything stupid. His door opens, and he disappears into the sky without leaving a trace.

I search the sky behind the car, looking for a hint of what's going on. The driver moves faster than before, speeding across the lake, and back into the city. Where is Celeste? From the look on Viktor's face, he's scared. Nothing scares him.

The car stops in front of the home I remember from the bad Viktor era. I hated this house and everything about it. The driver walks me to the front door, entering a code for the door to open. I turn toward the tall man, not sure who the hell he is or why he knows the code for Viktor's home?

"Have a good night, ma'am." He nods his head, ushering me inside. "I'll be outside if you need me."

"Are you some sort of security or something?"

"Or something," he answers, turning his back to me and heading down the narrow walkway.

I have no more answers than before. This cloak-and-dagger shit is getting old. I lock the door behind me and move away toward the infamous dining room. I'm shocked at what I see. The dark, terrifying haunted house that I remember from my nightmares has been completely remodeled with modern finishes. "What the hell?" The Gothic table that housed the horrors of the dinner parties and meals has been replaced with a farmhouse-style wooden table. I step back into the living room and realize the entire house has changed in the year since I've been here. When did he have this done?

I climb the twenty-six stairs to the stark white bedroom I once slept in. The door creaks open, revealing a room from a magazine. A large four-poster bed rests between two windows. Plush velvet covers match the hunter-green wallpaper covering the walls. "This is beautiful," I whisper to no one.

I make my way down to the library and the mess that Colby and I made while here. I flip the switch next to the door to a surprise. The mounds of dust that once covered the books are now gone. The organization that we tried to enact has been completed, along with a computerized card catalog. I walk through the room, rubbing my hands along the spines of the books. The once foreboding room is now warm and welcoming. The desk where Penelope's letters were found is gone, and I'm grateful, knowing it was just another part of this insanity.

"Amelia!" a familiar voice calls from another room.

"Celeste?" I call back, moving toward her voice. "Where are you?"

"In here!" she calls.

I move through the entire bottom floor of the house, not finding her anywhere. "Hello?" Something feels strange. "Celeste?" I call again.

"Amelia?" her voice calls from upstairs.

"Celeste? Fran?" This isn't right. Against everything inside me, I don't follow the sound of her voice.

"Where are you, Amelia?" she asks again. "I'm scared." I slide my new phone out of my pocket and text Viktor.

> Something is here.

> Go to the basement and hide. There's a safe room.

I head toward the kitchen, hoping the entrance to the basement is in the usual spot. I find a pantry, a garage, and a half bathroom, but no basement. "Shit," I whisper.

"Amelia?" the voice calls from the living area. I don't know what's out there, but I don't like it. "Amelia?" the voice has changed from Celeste to a guttural sound. Something large is knocked over and the sound of dragging moves closer to the door. I'm backed into a corner with nowhere to hide.

The swinging door to the kitchen opens, revealing a horribly deformed figure of a man. "There you are." He smiles a sickening smile. I know without asking he's a Strigoi.

"Leave me alone."

"Don't you want to feed off of me?" He moves closer, and I realize the dragging sound I heard was his leg. His ankle is bent sideways, and he's walking on the side of his foot. "My master said you might be hungry."

"Who's your master?"

"My master is the most perfect woman in the world. I know her as the love of my life, but I believe you will know her as Penelope."

"I never would have guessed." My words are laced with sarcasm. "Your master is a bitch and can kiss my ass."

The strigoi laughs, spitting liquid from his mouth. "She would most likely agree with you."

"Who were you imitating earlier?"

He smiles again, showing the two teeth left in his mouth. "I think you know who."

"Where is she?"

"Who?"

I turn and roundhouse kick him straight in the gut. He flies across the room, slamming into the swinging door with a thick thud. "I'll ask you one more time. Where is she?"

Blood pours from the half-dead man's mouth and ears. "I don't know who you're talking about," he coughs, spitting blood halfway across the room. I don't give him a chance to speak again. I wrap my hands around each shoulder, easily lifting him off the ground, and pull my hands apart, separating his body into two large pieces. He falls to the ground in a heap, an eternal smile plastered on his face.

It was a strigoi. I killed it.

Several minutes pass with no response.

Viktor? R U okay?

Again, several minutes pass, and an uneasy feeling forms in the pit of my stomach. Don't do anything stupid, Amelia. You promised. I walk around the body, heading back into the dining and living areas.

"Don't do it," I say out loud, trying to talk myself out of something I'll regret. "You'll only get in the way and be the damsel in distress. Stay here where Viktor told you to stay." I move to the front door, looking for the car that brought me here. To my surprise, I don't see it. I move to a window, finding the street empty. "Shit... don't do it."

"Fuck it." I run through the kitchen and over the body that blocks the door to the garage. Inside my two choices are a turquoise Camaro or an extra-large SUV. I choose the Camaro, finding the keys inside. I'm on the main street in a matter of seconds, pushing the car to speeds way too fast for city streets.

Dialing Violet's number, she answers on the first ring. "Amelia Renee Lockhart, where have you..."

"I need your help," I interrupt.

"Where?"

"The Mandeville house. Something's wrong."

"On my way." She hangs up without another word.

the girl in the photograph

VIOLET'S bright red SUV is parked a few blocks away from the house. She texted, telling me she was waiting for me in the car. I pull alongside, and she jumps into my passenger seat. She scrunches her nose. "Girl, is that smell you?"

"Probably. I'll explain later."

She clears her throat and wipes her eyes. "What's going on?"

"I don't know," I confess, pulling away from her car. "When we were coming back to the Mandeville house, Viktor started acting weird. He said to trust him and had the driver take me back to the city."

"Then, why the hell are we coming back?"

"When I got back to the house in the city, a strigoi was there."

Violet turns toward me. "Inside the house?" I nod. "How the hell did it get inside?"

"I don't know, but he told me Penelope sent him for me to feed from."

"Why do I feel like there's more to this story?

"Because there is." We pull to a stop a few blocks from the familiar home.

"There is someone here. I feel it." Violet closes the car door quietly. She covers her lips with her fingers.

"What do we do?" I whisper.

"Are you sure you want to do this?" she asks, moving in front of the car.

My thoughts flash to my tiny maker inside with whatever or whoever is there. "Is it Penelope?"

She shrugs. "I wouldn't recognize her energy. It's someone I don't know. But I can tell they're powerful."

"Shit, it has to be her. Celeste is inside." I wipe a tear from my cheek.

"All the more reason for you to stay out here. Viktor's not dumb. He's not going to risk something happening to Celeste." She pauses. "Don't take this the wrong way, but you're just another liability if you enter that house. Neither one of us can fight her. Whatever Viktor's doing, he doesn't need someone else to rescue."

Her words hurt because they're true. I wouldn't be any help inside that house. "I can't not try."

"Yes, you can," she whisper-yells. "You're doing what he needs by staying out of his way."

I wipe tears from my cheeks. "Sometimes I don't like you."

She nudges my arm with her elbow. "Especially when I'm spitting facts."

"Are we just going to wait?"

"That's exactly what we're going to do. We're going to trust Viktor," she answers.

"I don't want to leave," I whisper. She nods, heading to the passenger door and sliding inside. I do the same to the driver's seat.

"Tell me where you've been?"

"On a ship with Erick, a few miles out in the Gulf." Violet looks at me like I've lost my mind.

"Was this on purpose?"

"It wasn't a vacation cruise if that's what you're asking." I look down. "Penelope was the cruise director."

"Looks like we have some time. Fill me in." She crosses her arms, turning her entire body toward me.

"There's not much to fill in. I was dumb and tend to head into situations that I shouldn't."

Violet snaps her fingers, clicks her tongue, and points at me. "Exactly the reason we're not going inside."

I pull my phone out of my pocket, hoping to see a text from Viktor. Instead, I see one from Celeste. I sit up quickly, reading a line that confirms my fears.

Mother's here.

"What?" Violet asks. I hand her the phone, taking a deep breath.

"We're still going to stay here," she reminds me.

> Are you okay?

Several minutes pass before she responds.

> I don't like her.

> Yeah, me either.

> I know you're outside. So does she.

I show the phone to Violet. "Shit. Should we leave?"

She laughs. "There's no point. She probably sensed us miles before I sensed her. She's known we were here."

I slam my hands into the steering wheel, making the horn honk. "God, I hate this!" My phone rings with an unknown number. "Should I?" I hold the phone for Violet to see.

She shrugs. "I think we both know who it is."

"Hello?" I answer, putting the sound on speaker.

"Hello, yourself. I see you managed to get out of that horrible holding cell you were in. I do hope they find the person or persons who are responsible for such a horrible act."

"Why are you here?"

"Why am *I* here? I believe this is my family. Celeste has turned into such a lovely young lady."

"I'm not a young lady, and I'm not your family," Celeste retorts in the background.

Penelope laughs. "She's such a little tease. No wonder I let her father have her back." Her words bring anger to the surface. Violet places her hand on top of mine and shakes her head. "Anyway. I would like to invite the three of you inside." Penelope laughs. "I'll expect you in ten minutes." The phone clicks off.

"Three?"

"Ollie's parked not far behind us." I turn, looking for the blonde vampire.

"What is he doing here?"

"I asked him to come. I wasn't sure what we were about to get into when you called. He was at the house, and I asked him to come." Her words are laced with innuendos that I don't have time to explore at the moment.

Violet sends a text. Within seconds, Ollie is standing outside my window and tapping on the glass.

"This is going to be fun," he moans.

"For a serial killer, maybe." Violet and I exit the car and head toward the house. Ollie steps in front of us and knocks on the door.

The door creaks open, revealing a wide-eyed Fran. "Come in, please." Her words sound so formal. "Mr. & Mrs. Luquire are in the sitting room."

My heart jumps into my throat at her words. We

follow her into the main room where Viktor and Penelope are sitting side by side on a small settee. His arm is around her shoulders and her hand is wrapped around his thigh. What in the ever-living hell? "Oh, look, dear. We have guests."

Viktor nods at the three of us, refusing to make eye contact with me. "Welcome."

"Where's Celeste?" I ask.

Penelope flips her wrist. "She's around here somewhere. You know how children are." She motions to several seats in front of them. "Please, sit." I walk stiffly, following Ollie and Violet to a chair directly across from Viktor. He's looking everywhere but at me.

Penelope covers her nose. "It seems you haven't had a shower since the last time we met."

"Yeah, I apologize about that. The strigoi you sent interrupted my personal time." Violet snickers at my words.

"Oh, Viktor. I like her. She's spunky." Penelope turns back to me. "How *is* my pet?"

"Dead," I answer. "The last time I saw him, he was in two pieces and lying on the kitchen floor." Viktor looks down at my words. Whatever the hell he's doing that close to her, better be the beginning of some grand scheme. I glare at the male vampire across from me, daring him to look up and answer my unasked questions.

"He was getting close to death anyway. I'd imagine

he was an easy kill." Penelope scoots closer to Viktor, leaving barely any room between them.

"How's Josh?" I ask, trying to get on her nerves.

She giggles. "You'd have to ask Viktor."

"So, you two are together now?" Oliver asks.

"Who are you?" She smiles.

"Dr. Oliver Fitzgerald," he answers.

"Oh, you're a doctor?"

"Among other things." He smiles.

"And you?" She turns toward Violet. "You smell like Harrison."

"He was my maker," Violet answers. "Or at least until I killed him."

"Well, well. Aren't you feisty? I wanted to kill him for many years."

"I bet you did, Mrs. Chambers," Celeste says coming down the stairs.

Penelope turns, looking up the stairs. "There she is now, the little darling." Celeste slides to the other side of her father, holding one of the pictures she discovered with the children and Penelope.

"Does this look familiar?" she asks, pointing the photograph at Penelope.

"Oh, my. Yes, it does. Look at those darling children."

"Those darling children were donors, weren't they?" I look at my maker, not sure what she's doing.

Penelope laughs awkwardly. "Of their own

requests, some were. I would never feed on a child purposely. That would be cruel."

"That's never stopped you before," Celeste retorts. She holds up another picture. This one shows the close-up of the girl that is so familiar to me. "Recognize this little girl?" She flips through a few more photos. "She and her twin sister are in a lot of the photos."

"She looks familiar, but I can't place her."

Celeste shows another photo of the two girls. "Here they are a few years later. Amazing how they haven't aged in the years between the two photos."

"Oh, for crying out loud. What are you trying to say?" Penelope asks. Her patience for her daughter is completely lacking.

"Here's another. This one is ten years later, and instead of there being two girls, there's only one." Celeste shuffles through a few more photos. "Here she is fifty years later. What do you notice?"

Penelope pushes the photo away. "I'm not into playing games."

"I'd like to see," I say from across the room. Celeste hops down, bringing me the picture. It is the same young girl, but she looks older. Not like a middle-aged woman she should be, but an older teenager. "She's aged." I run my fingers over her face. "Not normal aging, but aged."

"Right," Celeste says, handing me another photo. "This one was taken last year." She hands me a photo of someone I recognize in an instant. "Opie?" I look at Celeste. "Is this Opie? The Opie I know?"

"Yes. She changed the spelling of her name over the years, but it's her."

"How is that possible?" I ask, looking between the photos. "She should be over a hundred and eighty years old. Opie doesn't look a day over forty."

"Voodoo," Celeste answers.

"How does voodoo keep her from aging?"

"Oh, goodness. Anyone else find this boring?" Penelope fakes a yawn.

"I find it quite interesting," Ollie answers. "What about you, Viktor?"

"Celeste, what does this have to do with your mother?" he asks. His choice of words makes me cringe. The doorbell rings on cue.

"There's our answer now." Fran opens the door and welcomes the visitor inside.

I look up to see Opie walk into the room. She looks right at Penelope. "Hello, *Mother*." She looks around at the room full of vampires. "This looks like some shit about to go down."

monster

"WHY ARE YOU HERE, ODILIA?" Penelope asks.

"I invited her," Celeste answers for her. "I felt it was important for her to be here. After all, you were her mother, of sorts." What the hell is Celeste talking about?

Penelope laughs. "I don't know what you're talking about, mon petit amour."

"You're not allowed to call me that." Celeste glares at her mother. Penelope holds up her hands in surrender.

"Allow me to elaborate. Oh, and by the way, my name is Ophelia now." Opie moves toward a bar cart in the corner of the room and pours herself a full glass of whatever alcohol Viktor has inside. Every eye in the room is on her, and she knows it. She takes her time choosing a seat, raising the tension in the room. "My twin sister, Dorothea Rae, and I were born in 1845 right here in New Orleans. Like most people of color born in the South, we worked for a rich family."

"The Chambers family," Celeste helps.

Opie toasts the air in Celeste's direction. "Yes, little ma'am." She turns toward Penelope. "They were horrible people."

Penelope slides forward in her seat. "I'm sorry. What does this have to do with anything?"

"Let her speak," Viktor hasn't said much, but his words carry a lot of weight.

"Most families were producing items such as cotton or tobacco. The Chambers family, they were different. They produced children."

"Did you say, children?" Violet asks.

"I surely did." Opie takes a swig of her liquid courage. "Children that were meant to grow up and become donors for their friends."

"You were raising donor children for vampires?" I can't keep my mouth shut.

"You make it sound like it was a bad thing." Penelope laughs. "These children were starving or worse. I saved them. I gave them a bed to sleep in and a roof over their heads. If it wasn't for me, most of them wouldn't have lived to see adulthood."

"Forgive me, I may be confused. Am I correct in thinking you believe raising them to be food for vampires was a *good* thing?" The look on Oliver's face matches his words. He's as disgusted as the rest of us.

"She did and still does," Opie answers.

"Don't look at me like that. These children were given a life of luxury. If it weren't for me, they would've died. I trained them to be the perfect donor."

Opie laughs. "The life of luxury. Is that what we're going to call it? I remember being beaten daily. I remember my blood being drained so often as a young child that there were days I couldn't open my eyes." She takes a drink. "Those children that you were 'saving,'" she uses air quotes, "were dying because of you. I watched you drain my sister to the point of no return."

"I don't know what you're talking about."

"Like hell, you don't," Opie retorts. "Dorothea died because you drained every ounce of blood from her body, all in the name of training."

"Oh, my God," I whisper. Viktor makes eye contact with me for the first time, and I feel sick to my stomach. "I'm so sorry, Opie."

"Me, too." She laughs and finishes her drink.

"You always were the dramatic one," Penelope retorts, making Opie laugh.

"Forgive me again," Ollie interrupts. "Did you say you were born in 1845?"

"Yes, sir."

"If you're not a vampire, how, may I ask, do you not look a day over thirty-five?"

Opie laughs. "I like you." She gets up, pouring herself another drink. "Before being purchased by the

Chambers family, my grandmother taught me many things. Voodoo was one of them."

"This is a spell?" Violet asks.

"A very powerful one. I kept both my sister and me young for many years. If we stayed young, we would never be sold for the highest price. We'd be safe."

"Until she drained her," Celeste fills in the blank from across the room. Damn, Celeste has no sympathy for her mother.

"Yes, little one. Until she drained her," Opie agrees. "For years I did yours and Harrison's bidding, following every rule and every demand out of fear." She looks at me. "I'm sorry, Amelia."

"Sorry for what?"

"The memories of Harrison that were stolen from you when you were younger. I'm the one who took those away from you."

My stomach turns at the thought. The memories that flooded my mind when I was in transition to vampire were full of Harrison and knowledge of what he was. Opie performed a spell on me, wiping those memories from my mind. I've never put the pieces together, until now.

"I'm done doing your bullshit, Penelope. You no longer own me." Opie sets her glass down, turning toward the door.

Penelope stands. "You're not going anywhere, you ungrateful little bitch. After everything I did for you and that stupid sister of yours, this is how you repay me?

Neither one of you were worth the money I spent on you."

"That's enough, Penelope," Viktor announces.

"Shut up, Viktor. I should've done this years ago." She flies at Opie, knocking her to the ground at vampire speed. Opie doesn't resist. Instead, she smiles as her throat is slit open, covering the floor in dark liquid.

"Thank you," Opie mouths as her eyes close, and her breathing stops. Oh, my God. I stare at the psychotic vampire in front of me. Her teeth are borne, and blood covers the front of her dress as she stares at the rest of us.

"What are you all staring at? She had to die. All those lies she was spewing. You just can't find good help these days." She attempts to wipe the blood stains from the front of her gown while smoothing out the wrinkles.

"Get out," Viktor says, moving in front of me.

"But we're getting along so well." She laughs.

"If you think for one minute that I could ever be with someone so vile, then you don't know me at all."

"Vile? I seem to remember you worshipping me when we were younger."

Viktor scoffs. "I never worshipped you. I loved you."

"Worship, love. They're all the same thing."

"Not to me, they weren't. Not to Celeste, they weren't. You took her from me, made me think Chamberlin had kidnapped you both, and all the time you went willingly."

"Nonsense, Viktor. I love you."

"You never loved me. The only person you've ever loved is yourself. How could you let him turn our daughter into an immortal child? You knew what it would mean for her to spend eternity trapped in a five-year-old body." Viktor's anger is evident from the look on his face.

"What can I say? A child needs her mother. Besides, I sent her back." The more she speaks, the more unhinged she sounds.

"I didn't need you," Celeste says, moving closer to her father. "I remember everything, *Mother*."

"Enough of this," Penelope interrupts her daughter.

"Let her speak. You deserve to know what *he* did to her, what *you* did to her." Viktor protectively wraps his arm around Celeste's shoulders. "I need to know what he did to her."

Celeste swallows deeply before speaking. "The pain was horrible. I didn't understand what was happening to me, and you didn't care." Penelope looks uncomfortable for the first time. "You let him feed from me. You let him turn me into an abomination. You let him do *unspeakable* things to me."

The look on Viktor's face is deadly. Clearly, Celeste has never told him the truth from that time of her life.

"Enough!" Penelope screams. The front door bursts open as a group of strigoi enters the house. This is the perfect description of "all hell breaks loose."

"Kill them all!" she screams over the screeches of

the monsters. They've lost any semblance of being human and resemble a corpse more than a human.

Oliver and Violet work as a team and kill two of the strigoi within minutes. Viktor grabs Celeste, pulling her toward the back of the house. In the moment I stop to watch, a strigoi is on top of me. Spit is dripping from his lips, and his fingers look more like claws than a hand.

"Bitch," he yells. "Stupid bitch!"

I recognize his voice instantly. "Josh?" I knock him to the floor. He jumps up, back on two feet.

"All you had to do was die!"

"Josh! You don't have to be this. We can help you. I can help you."

"I don't need help. Penelope loves me." He rushes me for the second time, and I knock him back easily.

"Yes, baby. I love you. Don't listen to her." Penelope screams from the other side of the room. Josh is the only strigoi still living. Violet and Ollie easily killed the others. I stare at the boy who was my friend.

"Don't make me do this," I beg. "I don't want to kill you." I look over, seeing Ollie and Viktor battle against Penelope. They're moving so fast that I can barely track their movements. Josh jumps on me for a second time, thrashing his teeth toward my neck.

"I'm going to kill you," he says, sinking his teeth into my throat and sucking. What the hell? I jump to my feet, throwing him across the room. He hits the wall with a sickening thud and runs straight toward me.

"I'm sorry, Josh." I reach my hand forward at the

same time he arrives in front of me, ripping his heart from his chest. His eyes enlarge and his pupils dilate as he falls to the floor in front of me.

The fight in the room rages on as more strigoi file through the front door. This time there are at least thirty and within minutes they have Violet and Ollie surrounded. Penelope steps back from the crowd. "Yes, my children. Kill them."

She turns, heading straight toward me. "You, my dear, are all mine."

"Leave me alone."

"Now, why would I do that?"

"Because you want to live," a deep voice says from behind me.

"Darling," Penelope answers in a singsong voice. "You know all I've ever wanted was to be with you. And it's obvious from this look-alike you brought in, you miss me. We can have that again. We can be a family, the three of us. I never wanted to be with Harrison. It was always you. It's always been you."

Viktor moves faster than I can track. Celeste disappears from behind me as he carries her out of the room and moves somewhere safe. He's back in the room and on top of Penelope in an instant. The two of them are fighting at supersonic speed while Violet and Ollie are still battling the new strigoi. Like the untrained fighter I am, I stand in the middle of the living room, watching everything happen in total confusion. What do I do?

"Get Celeste out of here," Viktor says, moving past

me. For once, I don't argue. I run out of the room, heading toward the basement. I'm sure that's where he stashed her.

"Celeste?" I call over the noise of the fight. Running down the stairs, I don't find her anywhere. The security room is locked. "Celeste!" Through the window I can tell the room is dark and empty. Where the hell is she? "Shit! Celeste! We have to go."

Where would she be? I turn to head up the stairs and see my worst nightmare waiting at the top. "We meet again," Penelope says with a sickening smile. Her face and clothes are covered with blood.

"Where's Viktor?"

"He's indisposed at the moment. He'll be back to normal within the next hour, I would think."

"What did you do to him?"

"Nothing he hasn't done to other people hundreds of times." She moves down the stairs, closer toward me.

"Leave me alone. I don't want to hurt you."

Penelope laughs. "Hurt me? That's cute."

"What's the purpose of all of this?" I ask, hoping to distract her long enough to escape.

"All what, dear?" She moves even closer.

"All of this, everything. Why get the cult organized? Why go after the family you abandoned? Why go after me?"

"Oh, that's easy. Because I can."

"You're crazy."

She laughs. "So, I've been told. Although, I will admit. I'm getting tired of this conversation."

"You're free to leave any time you want."

She flies across the room, knocks me to the floor, and straddles my hips. "It's time for you to die now." Penelope bares her teeth as she prepares to take my head.

"Mommy, stop." Penelope freezes in place.

"Celeste? What are you doing here?"

"I'll go with you, Mommy. Don't hurt Amelia." Celeste's voice sounds more childlike than I've heard for a while. "I forgive you, Mommy." For a brief moment, Penelope's eyes soften. "We can be the family we used to be."

Penelope relaxes her hold on me. "Like we used to be?"

"Yes, Mommy. Like it was before, when we were in France."

As quick as her eyes softened, they lose the brief glimpse of what's left of her humanity, and her grip strengthens. "That's sweet dear, but she can't live. We're vampires, this is what we do."

Celeste steps out from behind an old door, propped against the wall. "No, this isn't what we do. We love each other and treat each other with respect. We appreciate what others do for us, and we let them know how much we appreciate them."

"Aww, look at you with your morals. We'll have to change that." Penelope laughs a deep laugh.

"Celeste, go!" I manage to squeak out. She ignores me.

"Are you trying to protect *my* daughter from *me*?" She turns back toward me. "I would never hurt my child."

"It's too late for that," Celeste whispers.

Penelope wrinkles her forehead. "I'd never hurt you. How could you say such a thing? Everything I did was for your good."

"Nothing you did was for my good. You have to die."

"Fortunately, there's no one in this city who can make that happen."

"That's where you're wrong, Mommy." Celeste moves even closer. "There is someone."

Penelope laughs. "You must be privy to knowledge I don't have. Now, be a good girl, and go pack your clothes." Penelope turns her attention back to me. "I have something to finish up before we go."

In an instant, Celeste jumps on her mother's back, twisting her head backward, making them face-to-face. "That's where you're wrong, *Mother*. An immortal child, especially one that's seven hundred years old, is stronger than you'll ever be."

"You wouldn't hurt your mother. I'm the only one who truly loves you."

"When you get to hell, tell Harrison I said hello." Celeste rips Penelope's head from her body, letting it fall to the ground in a wet thud.

I stare at my tiny maker in awe. Her red curls are

covered in blood, along with her face and dress. She looks like she just stepped out of a horror movie.

"Celeste, are you okay?" I jump off the floor, moving in front of her.

She wraps her arms around my waist, pulling me close, and nods. "I'm okay. She's had it coming for a few centuries."

"Look at me." I pull away, putting my hands on her shoulders. She looks up, blood covering her cheeks. "You saved me. Thank you. I'm so sorry you had to do that."

She turns, looking at the remains of her mother. "She was never my mother, not in the true sense of the word." Wise words coming from a small child. Something large hits the floor above us. "We're needed upstairs." She grabs my hand, pulling me back into the middle of the fight. Dozens of bodies litter the floor while new ones keep piling through the door when we arrive back on the scene.

A dark blur stops in front of us, and Viktor picks Celeste up in one big scoop. "Why are you here?" he asks, looking around the room. "Where's Penelope?"

"Dead," Celeste answers. "I killed her."

He puts the tiny killer down. "Are you okay?"

"Why does everyone keep asking me that?" She turns toward the fight and transforms into something from a horror movie. Claws replace her fingers, and vampire teeth protrude from her mouth. This is what nightmares are made from. Without waiting for permission, she runs toward the fight, slicing her way through five strigoi without hesitation.

"Shit," I whisper, following Viktor into the fight. The three of us, along with Ollie and Violet kill the remaining strigoi in minutes.

Scanning the room for Celeste, I find her huddled in a corner, arms wrapped around her legs and rocking back and forth. "Celeste," I touch her shoulder. She growls as her head pops up, showing her teeth. "Celeste, it's me."

"Step back," Viktor warns, coming between us. "She's not in control right now." For the first time since meeting her, I see why immortal children are outlawed. I long to reach out, comfort her, and tell her everything's going to be okay. Instead, I stare at the tiny creature in front of me, and I'm scared. "Celeste," he whispers her name. "I'm here. Come back to me, mon petit amour."

Celeste growls and hisses, reminding me of an animal trapped in a cage. Tears stream down my face. I don't know how to help her. "What can I do?"

"Nothing. Stay back, and let her gain control. She has to overtake the vampire part of her." Viktor sits crossed-legged on the floor in front of her, holding her hands in his. She could easily overtake him, and he'd be dead within seconds. He begins singing in French. It's a song I don't recognize, but Celeste seems to. Her head pops up, and her breathing slows down. "Répondez moi plus tard," he whispers over and over. Her eyes slowly become more human, as her dilated pupils relax and form into a normal shape.

"Daddy," she whispers.

"I'm here, mon petit amour. I'm here." Celeste looks around the room at the blood and carnage.

"What happened?"

"We're safe." He stands, lifting her tiny body easily into his arms. "You're safe."

"Amelia?" Her head pops up, looking for me.

"I'm here." I move to their side, wrapping my arm around the two of them.

TWENTY-THREE

why am i so pissy?

IT TAKES hours to clear the house of all the bodies. Most are in pieces, which makes the cleanup last even longer. These bodies belong to strigoi, but they were once fully human with families and people who loved them. Now they're nothing more than a pile of debris next to the lake. Viktor hasn't said what the plan for them will be, and I don't ask. To be honest, I'm not sure I want to know. I haven't seen anything that I recognize as belonging to Josh, and I'm grateful. I don't know that I could handle that right now.

Fran took Celeste upstairs to rest after the fight, and Viktor hasn't said more than two words since. I don't know whether to comfort him or be pissed at him. I'm leaning toward being pissed. Images of his arm wrapped around Penelope and her cuddled next to him on the couch keep coming to mind. No doubt, he senses my anger. I've caught him watching me several times. I don't give him the benefit of acknowledging his stares.

"I think that's everything," Violet says. The two of us stare over the vastness of the lake, side by side. "That was some crazy shit."

"You can say that again." I turn toward my friend. "Thank you. We couldn't have done this without you."

She slides her arm around my back. "I don't think that's true. Celeste did most of the work. I've never seen an immortal child in action, and after that, I don't want to ever again. She was terrifying."

"I'm worried about her." I turn, looking behind me. Oliver and Viktor are nowhere around. "I have to protect her."

"Amelia, after what I saw, she doesn't need protection."

"Not from strigoi or lycan, but if word gets out that there is an immortal child alive, they could come."

Violet looks at her boot. "You're right. They will want her dead."

"I can't. I won't let that happen."

"Phillipe is the only other one who knows, besides Oliver," she reminds me.

Ollie walks out of the back door, carrying what looks like part of a foot, and throws it on the pile. "What are you two discussing?"

"How much we hate this," Violet answers. Ollie wraps his arm around her waist, and she leans into him. I feel my eyes enlarge.

"When did this happen?"

Violet laughs. "I don't know if it *happened*, but we've been spending a lot of time together."

"Ready to go?" Ollie asks her.

"Are we done here?"

"Aye. Viktor said there was nothing else we could do at the moment. There is a meeting scheduled for tomorrow to deal with the cult. With Penelope out of the picture, that should be an easy task."

Violet pulls away from Ollie's side and wraps her arms around my shoulders. "Everything is going to be okay."

I nod, wiping a tear. "Thank you, both."

"Anytime."

I stand by the shore, listening to the waves crash until the sun completely sets. Viktor hasn't come out of the house since they left, and I'm dreading going inside. Maybe I should just leave. To be honest, I don't know why I'm upset. Viktor and I were never a couple. In fact, we've spent most of the last year teasing each other relentlessly. He can be with whoever he wants to.

That thought makes the decision for me. Heading out the back gate, I move toward the Camaro at vampire speed. Thankfully, being in the middle of nowhere, the doors are unlocked with the key fob inside. No one has bothered a thing.

I jump inside and head across the lake as quickly as possible. My cell phone buzzes several times, and I ignore it. I don't know where I'm going, but I have to get away.

Half an hour later, I pull into the parking lot of the dorm. Sitting in the car, staring at the looming building in front of me, the emotion of everything that's happened hits me like a ton of bricks, and the tears flow uncontrollably.

The common room is empty when I enter. Ironically, the movie playing on the wall-mounted television is a vampire book turned into a feature film. I laugh as he sparkles in the sunlight before heading toward Josh's room. Roger needs to know his roommate won't be coming home. I knock on the door several times and sigh when there's no answer. It's a conversation I'll need to have, but I'm secretly grateful I don't have to do it tonight.

Heading upstairs, I'm surprised to find the door to my room cracked open. I open the door to find the room ransacked. "Seriously?" I stare in disbelief at the clothes, books, and shoes littered across the room. "What the hell happened?"

"Oh, my God. Riley? Is that you?"

I turn, seeing my RA in the door. "It's me. What happened to my room?"

"I don't know. I found it like this earlier. Do you know who would do this?"

"Sadly, yes. It's safer for you to stay in your room and lock the door. Even better if you can leave campus for a few days."

Samantha looks at me like I'm crazy. "It's finals week. I can't just leave campus. No one can. What's going on?"

"The people who did this are relentless, and they know who I am."

She cocks her hip to the side. "Who are you?"

"I'm a spy. I work for the government. The people who did this found out who I am."

"You're a spy? Does that mean Mr. Smith really isn't your uncle?"

Dear, lord. "No, he's not my uncle. Samantha, this isn't a movie. These people are dangerous. You and everyone on this floor need to stay safe."

"Okay," she answers, not hearing anything after, "He's not my uncle." I pull my phone out, ignoring the block of texts I've received since leaving.

> At Tulane. Dorm room was destroyed. Roger isn't here.

> Tulane? Why are you there?

> Is that important right now?

> I'm on my way.

> No. I'll meet you at the house in the Quarter.

He doesn't respond, and I'm shocked. "Did you just text him? Do you think I could have his number?"

I stare into Samantha's eyes. "Go to your room and lock yourself inside. It isn't safe for anyone to be out here."

Her pupils dilate, and her face becomes expressionless. "It isn't safe," she repeats. "I'm locking my door and staying inside." Did I just compel her to do something? I don't have time to figure it out. I lock the dorm room and head back toward the car. Instead of taking the Camaro I "borrowed," I choose my old Nissan, which is still parked in the back lot. I slide inside after pulling the five parking violations from the windshield and throwing them in the backseat.

Luckily, traffic is light, and I'm in front of the house in twenty minutes. Remembering the door code the driver used, I enter the quiet house. "Viktor?" I call through the rooms. The body of the strigoi is still lying in pieces all over the kitchen. After all the bodies we just cleaned up, I don't want to deal with this one right now.

The garage door opens, and Viktor walks in. "What's happened?"

"This is the asshole that tried to get to me earlier." I kick part of his leg.

"I mean at the dorm. What happened at the dorm?"

I shrug. "My room was destroyed, and Roger wasn't there. It has to be the cult." I cross my arms over my chest. "I don't know why I texted you."

"I'm glad you did."

"Well, I'm not. I don't know what the hell I was thinking." Stepping over the strigoi, I head into the sitting room.

"We need to talk," he announces, following me.

"Do we? I'm not so sure." Why am I being a bitch?

He moves in front of me, stopping me in my tracks. "We do. I'm sorry for what you saw." Dammit, I will not cry.

"What did I witness? What *was* that?"

"That was me trying to keep her there."

I turn, trying to move around him. "Certainly looked like you were successful."

"Amelia, stop." His hand wraps around my elbow, turning me back toward him. "I was going to kill her."

"With what, your dick? I mean, I don't have any first-hand experience with it, but I'd imagine it's possible."

"Don't be crude," he scolds, looking at the ground.

"Crude? Are you fucking kidding me? Crude? You let that bitch into your home. You let her touch you. You let her touch Celeste."

"I didn't let her in!" he yells. "She was there when we arrived earlier. That's why I sent you away. She had Celeste."

"What do you mean *had* Celeste?"

"Just what it sounds like. She had her tied up in her room. The only way she would agree to let her go was for me to come back with her and pretend to live as a family."

"Did you...did you make love to her?"

He sighs. "No."

"Did you want to?"

He moves away from me. "In the years since I lost her, I dreamed of finding her again. Prayed that her death was a hoax and that we'd be reunited as a family. The three of us, together again." He turns, facing me. "When I saw her again, I didn't want any of that."

"Then why pretend?"

"So, she would free Celeste, and because I knew you'd come. If Penelope for one minute thought I had feelings for you, she would've killed you on the spot."

I look up at his words. "What are you saying, Viktor?"

He turns, running a hand through his hair. "Hell, I don't know what I'm saying."

"I'll tell you." Using all my strength, I turn him around, facing me. "You are trying to blame your fucked up emotions on me. I get it. She's your wife. You've loved her for hundreds of years. But don't try to pin your confusion on me." I curse the tears ready to fall from my eyes.

"I'm not confused." His voice is no louder than a whisper.

"I think you very much are, and it's time for you to go or me to go. Or whatever." I head upstairs to the room where my clothes are. "I need a shower."

Viktor moves so fast; I can't track him. In an instant, I'm picked up and carried into his bedroom. He sets me down, pushing his body into mine, and backing me into a wall. "I'm not confused, Amelia. I know exactly what and *who* I want," he growls. His lips are on mine in an instant. The moment we touch, anger melts from my body, and I open my mouth, relenting to him. His tongue touches mine, and every cell in my body lights on fire. He lifts me off the ground, wrapping my legs around his waist as he carries me to the bed. In a flurry of movement, my shirt is in shreds on the floor, and my breasts are exposed.

"You are beautiful," he whispers, taking each nipple into his mouth. I don't hesitate to rip his sweater from his torso, exposing a six-pack of abs that have been hidden from view.

"What are we doing?" I ask, breathlessly.

"What I've wanted to do for a year." His mouth is on top of mine again as he slides the filthy jeans I'm wearing off my legs. I don't know how he did that without interrupting our kiss, but I'm impressed with his skills. "Is this okay?" he asks, pulling his pants down to his knees.

"It's more than okay," I whisper, bringing his mouth back to mine. He enters me, filling me to capacity, and I cry out in pleasure. His tongue matches the thrusting, and it doesn't take long before I can't control the fire building inside. One last deep pump has me screaming his name. He moans as loudly as I do before collapsing his body weight on top of me. We're both breathing harder than if we'd run a marathon.

I don't waste a minute. Using my strength, I flip him over, straddling his hips. His erection is still in place as I begin to slide up and down, eliciting moans from the vampire underneath me. Placing his hands on my thighs, he helps me move until we're moving in perfect unison. I feel the tension building, this time from deep inside. I reach around, taking the base of him into my hand and massaging as we join. Like before, we erupt at the same time.

We lay together for several minutes before either of us moves. Slow warm kisses gently cover my forehead and eyes. "That was better than I'd imagined."

"You've imagined this?"

"Many times," he confesses.

"Why didn't you tell me?"

He's quiet for a while. "After the things I did when we first met, I thought you would never be able to think of me any other way."

I lean closer, kissing him gently and sliding off of him. "I still think you're an asshole." I smile, moving off of the bed. "I need a shower before we figure out this cult shit."

"Are assholes welcome in the shower with you?"

"They are. Regularly, I might add." He smiles and follows me inside.

TWENTY-FOUR

knock, knock, greggie

ALL I HAVE to say is, thank goodness for a tankless water heater. Viktor and I stay in the shower until the sun peaks over the horizon. I've lost count of how many times and positions we've explored with each other since coming in here.

"I see the red of your hair peeking through the brown dye." He gently massages the shampoo into my hair for the third time.

"Yeah, I'm ready for it to go away." I turn facing the man who's had me in at least fifty positions and, from the looks of it, could go again easily. "As much as it pains me to say this, we need to get out of the shower and figure out what we're going to do about this cult." He moves behind me, wrapping his arms around my chest, placing a breast in each hand, and kissing my neck. His erection pushes against my ass, and I have to stop myself from reaching around and grabbing it.

"Are you sure we need to leave?" he whispers in my ear.

"No, but yes." He pushes into me from behind, bending me over to allow for easier access. I brace my hands on the wall in front of me, and he slowly slides in and out. "This is not leaving," I say, breathlessly.

"No, this is coming." He grunts his release, relaxing his head on my back. "I could do this all day."

I turn, facing him, and wrap my arms around his neck. His long hair has come out of its tie, and instead of the usual slick back style he wears, it hangs loosely to his shoulders. "You are hot like this."

"I'm not hot all the time?" he teases.

"No, not really. Most of the time, you look like a pretentious prick."

He laughs, lowering his lips to mine. He moans as I open my mouth for him. "Samantha doesn't think so."

I pull away. "Speaking of Samantha, after I found my room destroyed, I told her I was a spy, and that we worked together. Now that she knows you're not my uncle, she thinks you're free game."

"Good to know," he whispers into my mouth as he leans in for another kiss. I step out of the shower, grab a large fluffy towel, and leave him alone and erect.

"I'm going to get dressed. You might want to put that thing away." I stare longer than I should at the naked vampire in the shower.

"Your words are saying one thing, yet your eyes are saying another." He moves toward me, and I back out of the bathroom, running to my room. His laughter trails behind. It doesn't take long to find a pair of jeans and a T-shirt for the day. I towel dry my hair and get ready in record time. I sense Viktor before he knocks on my door. "Come in."

He's wearing a pair of jeans and a light blue Henley-style shirt, making his copper eyes pop. His hair is loose and hanging to his shoulders, and he resembles a supermodel more than an ancient vampire. "What's the plan, mon amour?"

"You come in here dressed like that, and you expect me to be able to function?"

"You like it? I'm trying to look more modern."

I step in front of him. "I like it." He kisses me on the lips. "The cult will be weakened without Penelope. Maybe they'll just disappear?"

"We should be so lucky." He pulls his phone out of his pocket, reading a text. "Oliver and Violet have called a meeting at The LaLaurie house for this morning."

"What time?"

"In an hour." He dials a number on his phone. Who the hell is he calling? "Hello, mon petit amour. How are you this morning?" The smile that covers his face at the sound of her voice makes my heart beat faster. "Good. I'm glad you're feeling better. I'm so proud of you." He wipes a tear from his cheek. "Yes, she's fine. She misses you." I blow a kiss toward the phone. "She sends her love." He pauses, listening. "Okay, I'll let her know. I don't know if she's going...okay. Okay. Okay...I'll tell

her. I promise. No, I promise," he argues. "I love you."
He hangs up the phone.

"What are you supposed to tell me?"

"Celeste insists that you be careful and not put yourself in harm's way." I laugh out loud.

"I'm in danger of being pounded to death."

"Pounded? Is that a new word?" He laughs.

"I'm surprised you haven't heard it on social media."

"I've been a bit preoccupied as of late." He wraps his arm around my shoulder and pulls me toward the door.

We manage to find a parking spot on the street, directly in front of the mansion, which is a springtime miracle. The house doesn't look quite as menacing as it once did. We enter the code and walk inside. This time no tourists follow us in, and I'm grateful. "Hello?" a voice calls from the back.

"Erick?" I answer, recognizing his voice.

"Amelia?" A dark figure zooms in front of me, and arms wraps around me. "You look beautiful this morning, my dear. Your cheeks are simply glowing."

I pull away from our embrace. "You look better than the last time I saw you."

"I smell better, too. You smell like..." Viktor clears his throat. Erick laughs, turning toward Viktor. "Good morning, Luquire."

"Comstock," Viktor retorts.

The door opens as Ollie and Violet enter. Erick moves toward them, greeting Violet with a sexy kiss on the cheek and a longer-than-usual hug. "He's a flirt," Viktor whispers.

"I am not a flirt. I enjoy women. There's a difference." Erick shakes Ollie's hand, introducing himself just as Phillipe walks through the door. He stops dead in his tracks, staring at Erick.

"You're alive?"

Erick smiles wide. "I am, my friend." The two men embrace, patting each other on the back as only men can do. "You look good."

"As do you." He looks at the rest of us. "Where's that little shit, Brian?"

"He wasn't invited," Violet answers. "Oliver and I felt like this conversation would be better off without him."

The small group moves to the conference table in the back room. Everyone takes their seat at the round table. "I feel like one of King Arthur's knights." Everyone stares at me deadpan. "What?" I look around the room. "None of you are old enough to have known him. Are you?"

Erick laughs and turns to Viktor. "You're the oldest."

Viktor laughs but doesn't answer. "Let's get to the matter at hand. The cult." He reaches over, taking my hand into his. "With Penelope dead, their leadership should falter, and their existence dissolve."

"Penelope's dead?" Erick is the first to speak. "When and how?"

"She broke into my home, and I killed her." No one contradicts him. The three of us who know the truth would never put Celeste's life in danger.

"She's really dead?" Phillipe asks. We all nod. "Then why are we meeting?"

"After we left your house last night, Ollie and I did a little investigating. We found the headquarters of the cult and paid their leader a little visit." Violet stands from her chair, walking around as she speaks.

"You did what?" I'm not sure I heard correctly.

"Greg wasn't too pleased to see us, but Ollie changed his mind." Ollie flashes his teeth.

"God, I would've loved to have seen that."

"I got it on video. I'll show you later." Violet smiles, wiggling her phone at me.

"What happened?" Viktor interrupts.

Ollie stands, moving next to Violet. They share a look. "They were talking to Penelope, but we don't think she was the one in charge."

"What do you mean?" Viktor stands, moving closer to the duo.

"He means we think someone else was in charge. Someone more powerful. Someone older."

"That's not possible," Erick answers. "There is no one more powerful or older. Hell, I don't know of anyone in America that's older."

"We don't think they're in America."

It's Phillipe's turn to stand. "What would an ancient vampire from another country want with New

Orleans and controlling the vampire and wolf population?"

"That's what we don't know," Violet answers.

"Where is Greg?" Viktor asks.

Oliver slides a piece of paper with a handwritten address across it. "He lives in the Quarter."

"Let's go pay this Greg guy a visit," Erick says, moving toward the door.

We pile into the back of Erick's extra-large SUV and follow the directions to a small apartment building a few blocks away. The humor isn't lost on me, that an SUV full of six vampires is driving through the streets of New Orleans on the way to terrorize a chubby, psychotic human.

"Shall we all go up?" Erick asks.

"I think we shall," Phillipe answers. "The more the merrier."

Viktor leads the way up the stairs to an apartment on the top floor. "Ooo, can I be the one he sees when he opens the door?" I slide in front of Viktor.

"Of course, mon amour." I knock gently as the rest of the crew moves out of the way of the peephole.

"What?" Greg's sharp voice sounds through the door.

"Greg? It's Riley. I need your help. I think a vampire is following me." Someone snickers behind me.

"Riley?"

"Yea, from the meetings. I was Zoe's friend."

I hear what sounds like four or five door locks click,

and he cracks the door open. "Now's not a good time, Riley. We have a meeting tomorrow night. Why don't you come? We can talk then."

"I'm really scared." I look around, doing my best job of acting.

"How'd you find out where I live?"

"Zoe told me." Greg looks like he's thinking about my response but doesn't question it. Someone bangs on the downstairs door, making him jump.

"I'm going to close the door. Goodbye, Riley."

"No, wait." I stop him from closing the door, slamming it into him as the six of us pile into his house. Oliver closes the door behind him.

"What...what are you all doing here?" he stutters over his words.

"We think you have information that needs to be shared." Violet steps forward. "Remember me?"

Greg stumbles backward, tripping over his own feet. "What do you want with me?"

"She just told you," Viktor says, moving closer. "Penelope's dead."

"What? She's dead?" He sits heavily on the polyester couch, straight out of the '60s. "How?"

"How isn't important." It's Phillipe's turn. "She's gone which means this bullshit you're doing is over. Do we make ourselves clear?"

Greg buries his head in his head and sobs. "How can she be dead? We were going to be married. Oh, Penelope, my love."

I can't control the laughter. "You and half of New Orleans probably thought the same. She was using you, Greg. You fell for it hook, line, and sinker."

Ollie steps forward. "Was she the only one in charge?"

"I...I don't know what you're talking about." He jumps to his feet, moving away from our group. "Penelope was the only one I talked to, I never talked to..." He stops himself.

"Never talked to who, Greg?" Erick steps closer. I love how we're tag team scaring the shit out of this dickwad.

"I don't know any names."

"What did Penelope say about them?" Viktor asks.

"Only that they were coming, and when they got here, they wanted everyone dead. Wolf and Vamp." The front of Greg's gray sweatpants is soiled with urine.

Violet is the first to act. She moves toward him so quickly he nearly falls over. She grabs him around the neck, lifting him off the ground and slamming his back into a wall. "What was the name?"

Greg kicks his feet, holding onto her arm. "Penelope called them, her maker." Violet releases her hold, and he slides down the wall like a cartoon character.

I turn toward Viktor. "Her maker?"

"What does that mean?" Ollie asks.

"It means we're fucked," Violet answers.

Viktor wraps his hand around my arm, leading me to the door of the apartment. He turns toward the quartet of vampires in the room. "He can't leave this room." They nod in unison as Viktor pulls me down the stairs and outside.

"What's going on?"

He runs a hand through his hair. "Her maker is my maker." I nod, remembering the story he told me.

"Okay, and?"

"If she's coming here, it can only mean one thing."

He walks in circles. I've never seen him this out of control before. "Viktor, stop. What does it mean?"

"It means she knows about Celeste and is coming to kill her. This whole thing has been a distraction, and I fell straight into the trap."

"Then why are we just standing here? We need to get to the house and to Celeste, now." Viktor wraps his arm around me and lifts me off the ground. I don't know how he flies, but within minutes we're standing in the front yard of the Mandeville home. Viktor's body language has changed. He's frozen in place.

"What is it?" I ask the catatonic vampire next to me.

"She's gone," he whispers. "Celeste is gone."

i've never seen him like this

"WHAT DO YOU MEAN, she's gone?" I'm hoping I misunderstood.

"I mean, she's gone. I don't feel her, and she's not responding through our connection." He runs inside, leaving me trailing behind. He's standing in the door-frame of her bedroom when I find him. The house has no evidence of the bodies that littered the floor hours earlier. "I don't want to go in." His words are no louder than a whisper.

"Do you mind if I do?" He shakes his head. I squeeze past him and head straight toward her desk. Her room is perfectly neat, nothing looks out of place. I carefully open each drawer, looking for any clues.

"What's going on?" Fran asks, stepping behind Viktor.

"Where is she?" Viktor turns on her, anger filling his voice. "She's gone. What do you know?"

"Gone?" Fran turns toward the room. "She was downstairs a few hours ago. She's probably outside."

"She's not outside."

Opening the center desk drawer, I find a small puzzle box. "What's this?"

"She was always...always building those things." Viktor stutters over his words. "She went through a phase where all she did was build them."

"Show me how it works."

"Amelia, now isn't the time." He steps into her room, opening one of her closets. He pulls everything off the top shelf, looking for any clues to where she's gone. His movements have become frantic. The moves of a terrified father.

"Let me help." Fran moves beside him, picking up the pieces he's throwing. I stare at the puzzle box, shifting it around in my hands. Something about this box is drawing my attention. Viktor has moved on to one of her dressers, sorting through clothes and throwing them on the floor. "Sir, you're not going to find her in these drawers."

Studying the box, I slide a small piece of wood on the bottom over, separating it from the side. When it moves, a small drawer pops open. Inside is a folded piece of paper. I open it, finding a sequence of numbers written in what I assume is Celeste's handwriting. "What's this?" I ask over the commotion on the other side of the room. Viktor is busy destroying the room with Fran steadily picking up behind him. Neither is paying attention to me.

"Viktor! What is this?" He turns, taking the paper from me. "It was inside the box."

"It's just a bunch of numbers."

"May I?" Fran takes the paper, studying the writing. "When Celeste was working on her computer science degree, she spent a lot of time with encryption codes."

"You think this is some sort of encryption? What would be the purpose of that?" Viktor asks. "She wouldn't need to encrypt information from me."

"No, but she might need to encrypt it for others who might be looking for her." I open her laptop, hoping for more clues. "Shit. Does anyone know her password?"

Viktor sits and begins typing, immediately locking up the computer. "Sir, stop, please. I know her password."

I put my hand on his shoulder. "Viktor, I know you're upset. We all are, but you're not helping her or yourself unless you settle down. Panic is not going to help."

He slides back on her desk chair and takes a deep breath. Fran types in a series of numbers and letters. The computer comes online. The screen opens immediately, displaying a letter full of zeros and ones. "What is this?" Viktor stares at the screen.

"Don't touch it," I warn. "If you type something

wrong, it could clear everything, and we'd have no way of getting it back. This is coding."

"You're not speaking a language I understand." Viktor runs a hand through his hair.

"I don't understand it either, but I did have a course in coding for my undergraduate." I look at the folded paper I found inside the puzzle box. "I think this is the key to understanding this code."

"Dammit, why'd she have to make it so difficult? I don't understand this being so secretive. Who in the hell did she think would be in her room?" As soon as the words leave his mouth, the realization hits. He turns toward Fran.

Fran backs away from the desk. "Sir, I would never betray you or Celeste. I love her like my own."

"Leave," he answers.

"Mr. Luquire?"

"Leave now, before you're unable to." She backs out of the room, tears filling her eyes. "I would never harm her." She turns, running down the stairs and through the front door.

"Viktor? You don't think Fran had anything to do with this, do you?"

"If Celeste had reason to run and hide this letter, there was a reason. Out of the three of us in this room, she's the odd man out." He pulls the laptop off the desk, handing it to me. "Can you figure this damn thing out?"

"Give me a few minutes." I study her code not sure

where to start. "I have an idea." Entering the numbers from the puzzle box paper into the first line of the letter, the code takes shape and changes from numbers to words, taking the form of a letter. "I got it." He's by my side in seconds.

"What is it?"

"A letter. Want me to read it?" He nods.

> *Daddy and Amelia,*
> *First thing, I'm fine. I left of my own free will. No one forced me or vampire-napped me. Don't be angry, and know that I'm safe. Daddy, promise me you won't hurt Fran.*
> *Amelia, make him promise.*

"I promise," he whispers. Tears fill his eyes.

> *You better have promised. Fran had been in contact with Penelope for the past few months. I found their communications on her phone. Fran thought she'd hidden them, but I found them easily. Someone is coming, Daddy. They're coming for me, and Mother told them where to find me. She didn't want*

to become a family again. She only wanted to save herself.

"I'll kill her," Viktor says. Anger pouring from him.

You promised, Daddy. I know what you're thinking, and no. You can't hurt Fran. She's tired. Being a vampire isn't for the weak. Especially when your family and loved ones have long since died. And no, killing her won't be an answer to her prayer. She didn't and doesn't realize they're after me, but I do.

Immortal children are not allowed and not only my life will be taken. So will yours and Amelia's. I'm not going to be responsible for your deaths, not when I can do something about it. For that reason, I've left. Don't try to find me. I'll be in touch when necessary. Take care of each other, love each other, and know that I'll be safe. I'm doing this for us. I have a plan and a contact. Trust me.

I love you both,

Celeste

Viktor throws the laptop across the room. "Dammit! We could've fixed this together. She's five years old, for God's sake. She's not even old enough to get on a plane by herself."

I stare at the laptop, laying in pieces on the floor. This feels like a nightmare I'm unable to wake up from. I don't say anything to Viktor. Nothing I say will do any good.

"How the hell can I fix this?" he says, moving across the room.

"You can't."

"I will not accept that!" he yells. "She's my child, my baby. I will not stand by while she puts her life in danger."

I move closer to him. "She's your child, but she's anything but a baby. She's more capable than anyone I know. Where would she go?"

"I have no idea," he admits. "She could be anywhere in the world."

"We have to trust that she'll be okay. She knows what she's doing."

"How in the hell am I supposed to do that? I've spent my life taking care of her."

"That's why she left. She didn't want you to be responsible."

"That's not her choice," he cries.

"It's very much her choice."

I pick up the pieces of the laptop and place them on her desk. I don't know how Celeste plans on staying in contact, hopefully, it's not through her computer. There are no words adequate enough to heal his broken heart. I wouldn't even try at the moment. Instead, I leave him in her room to be alone with what's left of his daughter. I can't imagine the pain he's going through. I'm heartbroken, and I've only known her for a year. He's had a thousand years with her.

I'm surprised to find Fran downstairs, in tears. "You didn't leave?"

"I don't have anywhere to go. Celeste is my life."

"Is it true?" I sit across the room from her. "Were you working with Penelope?"

She buries her face in her hands. "I didn't realize it was her I was communicating with."

"How does that happen, Fran? You understand why that's not believable."

"I do," her voice is no louder than a whisper. "I would never betray Mr. Luquire or Celeste. I love her like she's my own."

"Explain it to me."

She pulls her phone out of her pocket. "I received a text from someone who I thought was a friend from the old country. A vampire. Turns out it wasn't him."

I stare at the woman sitting across from me. "Seriously? Do you realize how that excuse sounds?"

"I do now. I was lonely and..."

"The whole fucking time you were telling Penelope details about Celeste, about Viktor, about me?"

"No, I would never share private information. We never discussed them or you." She wipes tears from her cheeks. "Celeste is really gone?"

"I'm afraid so."

"How can I help?"

"You can't. You need to leave. Go to one of the other houses."

Fran stands, handing me her phone. "I don't want anything to do with modern technology. Look over the messages. You'll see I'm not lying."

"I'll be in touch."

She heads toward the door. "Find her, Amelia. Find her, please." She leaves, closing the door behind her.

Looking through Fran's phone is like searching my grandmother's iPhone. There's not even a passcode. I read through all of her text messages, which aren't many. Her text thread consists of a daily word of encouragement, texts from Celeste, and the number that belongs to Penelope, or someone she's working with.

Fran's right when she says the texts are harmless. There's nothing here that would give any information about Celeste, at least that I can see. I decide to send the number a text to see if they'll respond. If it's Penelope, she's obviously "away from her phone." I smile at the irony.

> How's the weather today?

That's a harmless enough text. I stare at the phone, willing someone to respond. I don't know what to do. I've never had the type of personality that sits around, waiting to be told what to do. I'm a go-headfirst type of personality. Sitting here, not doing anything, goes against every part of my being.

My phone buzzes with a text from Violet.

> What's going on?

I don't know how much Viktor will want to share.

> Celeste isn't feeling well.

I lie.

> We took care of Greg. The cult should be finished.

> Good. I'll let Viktor know.

Viktor comes out of nowhere, covering my mouth with his hand and turning me toward him. I open my eyes wide, hoping he'll understand I'm asking, *"What the hell?"* He raises a finger to his lips, giving me the universal sign for *"be quiet."* I nod.

"Hide, Amelia." I hear Celeste's voice in my head as

clearly as if she were standing next to me. *"Dammit, Amelia. Hide! Do it now!"*

I question my sanity but run to the kitchen, hiding behind the swinging door. The doorbell rings the instant I close the door. Cracking the door enough to peek through, I can tell even from here Viktor is nervous. *"Celeste?"* I scream through my mind. There's no response.

Viktor opens the door. "Hypatia. It is good to see you. I hope you are well."

"Hello, Viktor. You're not going to invite me in?" a female voice asks. I crack the door enough that I have a straight view of the front door.

"Of course." He laughs awkwardly. I've never seen him like this. He seems out of sorts and not like himself. He opens the door, and a young girl with bleached blonde hair enters. She's no taller than me and looks several years younger. Her hair is separated into two braids, each hanging on the side of her face and halfway to her waist. Her blood smells familiar and ancient.

"You can come out!" She yells toward the kitchen. "I know you're hiding behind that door."

Shit. Do I come out or stay hidden? "Amelia?" Viktor calls, answering my question.

I walk into the sitting room and wave at the young girl. "Hi, I'm Amelia."

"I know." She smiles. "Join us, please."

The tension in the room is palpable, and I don't

understand why. I look between the two of them, hoping one of them will offer an explanation.

"Amelia, this is Hypatia."

I smile. "It's a pleasure to meet you, Hypatia."

"Likewise," she answers.

"How do you two know each other?"

"Hypatia is my maker."

TWENTY-SIX

two months later

LIONS, TIGERS, AND BEARS...AND VAMPIRES

MY EYES open to the small closet I spent every night inside as a young child. It smells the same as always. A mixture of mold, dust, and home. The cardboard sheet I used as a desk is propped against the back wall, along with a small stack of library books I've borrowed to read.

"Amelia? Can you hear me?" Celeste's voice rings through my mind.

"Yes. Are you here?"

"No." Her voice sounds sad.

"Am I really hearing you?" I ask, not sure if I'm imagining hearing her voice.

"Because I'm your maker, I can talk to you through our connection. We're blood-bound."

"I miss you."

"I miss you, too," she answers. *"I'm close to discovering the answer, Amelia."*

"What answer? Celeste? What answer?"

"Amelia?" a deep voice sounds through my mind. "Are you listening? Amelia?"

I turn toward the voice. "Yes, I'm listening," I lie.

Viktor slides back in his chair. "What did I say?"

Shit. "You said Hypatia wants to go to Café du Monde later this evening?"

He stares at me dumbfounded. "Really? That's not even close." He sighs, crossing his long legs. "I was asking if you'd heard from Celeste today."

I sit up, sliding my feet underneath me. Since Celeste left, she's been in contact with me periodically in my mind. Hearing that his daughter is alive and communicating with me has helped ease Viktor's turmoil. "She was speaking to me just now."

"Really?" He smiles. "Is she okay? What did she say?"

"She sounded like usual. I told her I miss her, and she said she was close to discovering an answer."

"An answer to what?"

I shrug. "She never said."

"I wish she would talk to me." His voice sounds sad.

I move to his side, take his hand into mine, and kiss the back. "Celeste is brilliant. She knows what she's doing."

"I know. Still doesn't make it any easier." The doorbell rings, drawing our attention to the present. "Shit," he whispers.

"I can hear you," Hypatia's voice sings through the

door. "Today is zoo day!" Viktor shoots me a look and rolls his eyes.

"Yay," he mouths silently.

Tired of waiting on us, Hypatia opens the front door, letting herself in. She's wearing a pair of cutoff jean shorts, a crop top, oversized sunglasses, and a wide-brimmed hat. I still don't know the exact age of the ancient vampire, but she's older than Viktor and much older than the teenager she appears to be. "What's up, bitches?" she announces, coming into the room.

"Hello, Hypatia," Viktor welcomes. "Are you sure we need to accompany you to the zoo?"

"Please." She smiles weakly. "I do find these things boring to do alone." Her accent is a mixture of French, Scottish, and California teen. "It's been ages since I've been in New Orleans. You know what they say. When in New Orleans, do what the New Orleanians do...or something like that."

"I don't think that's what *they* say," I retort. Hypatia turns toward me with a glare. "Or maybe I've just never heard it that way before." I smile, swallowing my words.

"Feel free to stay home, Amanda. Viktor and I will hit the town alone."

"Amelia," I correct. "No, I'd love to come. Thank you for the invitation." Hypatia doesn't look overly excited at my announcement.

"Suit yourself." She turns toward Viktor, who's

wearing skinny jeans and a fitted sweater. "Are you wearing that? It's summer. Put some shorts on or something. You're dressed like a vampire."

"I am a vampire and not a huge fan of wearing shorts." A silent conversation seems to take place as Hypatia stares at him until he leaves the room, heading upstairs. Can he hear her in his head like I hear Celeste? I make a mental note to ask later.

"Have you been to a zoo before?" I ask, trying not to come across as awkward as I feel.

"Not this one, but I've been to several zoos before."

"When was the last time you came to the city?" I'm struggling to fill the void of conversation suppressing the room.

Hypatia sighs, putting her hands on her hips. "I guess around two hundred years ago. Of course, it was nothing like it is today." Thankfully, Viktor comes down the stairs wearing a pair of plaid shorts and a soft pink button-down shirt, interrupting my weak attempt at entertaining his maker.

"Is this better?" He does a catwalk spin when he reaches the landing. It takes every fiber of my being to hold the laughter inside. He's clearly miserable and looks like a tourist from the Midwest.

Hypatia claps her hands. "Yes! Let's go. I'll drive." We follow her outside to the car she purchased after arriving in the city, a hot pink Volkswagen Beetle.

"I'm not sure we're going to all fit. Why don't we take one of my vehicles?" Viktor encourages.

"Nonsense. This car has plenty of room. Amelia can crawl into the backseat." Viktor slides his seat forward, giving me barely enough room to squeeze into the car. The backseat is definitely made for looks, not comfort. Even with my short five-foot frame, my legs are squished into my body, and my knees are under my chin. This is great.

Hypatia zooms the car through the neighborhood and onto the bridge over the lake. "Isn't this great? Three vampires out on the town." Neither of us comments as we continue across the lake and into the city. Not only does she look like a teenager, but she drives like one who's just gotten their license. She whips the car into a parking place near the front entrance, throwing me across the tiny backseat and into a side window. "We're here! Audubon Zoo! What a fun name."

I slide out of the backseat, grateful for the fresh air and the ability to stretch my knees straight. We pay and enter with all the other poorly dressed tourists. "What is your favorite animal?" I ask, attempting to make conversation.

"The monkeys," she answers. "We don't have monkeys in France. I think they're hilariously funny with their tiny little fingers and tails. What's yours?"

"I've always been a fan of the peacocks. I know they're not in a cage, but their feathers and calls are beautiful."

She turns toward Viktor. "What about you?"

GARDEN OF MYSTERY AND INTRIGUE

"The elephants," he answers. "I don't know why."

We walk through the zoo, visiting each animal as she makes sure to read their sign aloud for everyone around us to hear. When we get to the monkey enclosure, it's clear they're her favorite. She spends time talking to each monkey, making sure to point out examples of each species and speaking to them like they're toddlers.

"Get out of here, abomination!" a woman screams from behind. Viktor and I are listening to Hypatia explain why the lemur monkey has a long tail when the scream comes again. "I'm talking to you! Get out of here, abomination!" I turn, facing the scream, not sure exactly what or who I'm hearing. "You're not welcome here, demon," she screams once more.

I nudge Viktor's thigh. "I think she's talking to us." He turns toward the woman.

She gasps, covering her eyes with her hands. "Filthy demons! You're an abomination! I can't look at you." Viktor moves closer. The woman is clearly shaking but doesn't back down. "You can't have my soul, shadow walker."

He takes the woman's hand into his, pulling it to his lips and kissing it gently. She looks nervous. "You are lovely. What is your name?" He lifts her chin upward and looks the woman in the eyes.

"Mary. My name is Mary."

"Mary," her name rolls off his lips in a hypnotic tone. "A lovely name for such a lovely woman."

She smiles and her body relaxes. "Demon," she whispers as he kisses her hand again.

"Mary, it's been a pleasure to meet you. Thank you for supporting the city of New Orleans." Mary actually giggles. "It's time for you to leave the zoo and go home to your family." His voice is kind and persuasive as he speaks.

"It's time for me to go home," she repeats. "I need to see my family."

"That's a good girl." He kisses her hand once more as she turns away, leaving us behind.

"What the hell was that?" I ask, watching the woman walk away.

"That was the power of persuasion," Hypatia answers. "I haven't seen you in action for a while, Viktor. You've developed your skills well." She sits on a nearby bench. "Does that sort of thing happen regularly?"

"No. That's the first time I've ever been approached by someone." He sits next to her.

"How did she know we were vampires?" I ask, not sure what just happened.

"I don't know that she knew what we are or just knew we were something," he answers.

"Well, now that she's gone, let's continue our day, shall we?" Hypatia stands, clapping her hands together.

We spend the next few hours exploring every cage, every crevice, and every enclosure, looking at creatures from around the world. As much as it pains me to admit it, I am enjoying the day. For the first time since Celeste left, I allow myself to have a good day. I squish into the back of the pink bug, and Hypatia steers us out of the parking lot. "I have one more stop before I take you back."

I can physically feel Viktor's eyes roll from the backseat. A few minutes later, we enter the French Quarter. "I love the historical feel of these streets. It reminds me of home." She keeps driving, turning into the Garden District. I'm not sure why she took the long way to get there, but I don't question her. She pulls onto a familiar street, and what used to be Harrison's house looms in the distance. Since Violet's taken it over, the gloomy feel it once had has gone, replaced with a more comfortable vibe.

Hypatia stops the car in front of the home, turning toward Viktor. "What happened to him?"

"Harrison?"

Viktor looks nervous. "He was killed."

"Who killed him?"

"One of his children." Children? Is that what they call the ones they turn?

"Why?" she persists.

"He was evil. His child killed him to save a human." I watch as Hypatia transforms into something from nightmares. The innocent exterior she's put on display has changed into a deformed creature with pointy ears, fingers, claws, and gray skin. She's terrifying.

"He was killed to save a human?"

281

To his credit, Viktor keeps his composure. "He was."

"Who was this human that was special enough to murder one of my children?" Viktor doesn't answer. "Don't make me repeat myself, my child. I could do things to you that would keep you from returning for months, even years. Answer the question."

"It was me!" I shout from the backseat. Viktor's eyes close at my admission. "I'm the human that was saved."

Hypatia turns toward me. "What would justify killing my child for you?"

Avoiding making eye contact with her, I look at my knee that's less than a foot from my face. "I don't know."

She grabs my head, pulling my neck toward her face. Instead of biting, she sniffs loudly. "That would explain why you smell like him."

"Hypatia, stop," Viktor pulls her attention away from me. "Amelia had nothing to do with his death. She was next to death herself."

"Who's her maker, Viktor?"

"I am," he lies.

Hypatia releases my head, throwing my whole body back in the seat. "Do you think I'm stupid? Who is her maker?"

"Violet is my maker," I announce. "That's why you smell Harrison. He was her maker."

"Where is this, Violet?"

"Is that why you're here, Hypatia? Is that the reason for this unexpected visit?"

"You'll do well to remember your place, Viktor. Remember when you came crawling to me, begging me to turn you into a vampire? I took pity on you then, but do not mistake that act of kindness for today. Tell me where to find Violet."

"She's gone."

"Where?" she asks.

"She sent me a text a few days ago, telling me she would be out of the country for a few months."

"Is this the truth?" she asks Viktor.

"Yes," he whispers. "It's the truth."

Hypatia turns back into the blonde-haired, blue-eyed teen she was earlier. "Okay, good. I'm glad we got that out of the way. Would anyone like to go hunting? I'm rather parched."

Viktor opens the door and literally pulls me from the backseat. "We'll find our own way home. Thank you for the day, Hypatia. Have a good evening."

She rolls down the window. "Are you sure you're not hungry? You know that goat shit is bad for you."

"We're good, thank you."

"Your choice." She starts to roll up the window, stopping midway. "Oh, I almost forgot. The council has given you four months to take the immortal child you've been hiding to the council seat and relinquish her there. Have a good night!"

I stare dumbfounded at the bright pink beetle

making its way down the road and out of the Garden District. "What the hell was that?"

"That was Hypatia in all of her glory."

"Do you think she knows about Celeste?"

He runs a hand through his hair, a very human movement. "That's the only reason she would show up like this. Dammit."

"Do you think that's why she left? Could Celeste have known something like this was going to happen?"

"I don't know." He turns, walking circles across Violet's yard. "I need to talk to her. I need to talk to my daughter."

I resist the urge to try and calm him down. I've seen Viktor angry, but not to this extent. I know without asking there's nothing he wouldn't do to protect his child.

TWENTY-SEVEN

WE PULL in front of the Mandeville house an hour later, after Viktor called an Uber. The humor of two vampires calling for an Uber to take them across the lake isn't lost on me.

"This house is beautiful," the young driver announces from behind the steering wheel.

"Thank you. I added a tip," Viktor says, stepping out of the car.

"Wow! Thank you, Mr. Luquire. Anytime you need a driver, please ask for me."

Viktor collapses on the couch the moment we're inside. "I don't know what to do. For the first time in a long time, I don't know how to fix this."

"Maybe it's not something that you can fix." I sit next to him, wrapping my arm through his.

"If Hypatia knows about Celeste, the council knows.

285

They will kill Celeste. They're not interested in anything other than she's an immortal child and therefore must die."

"We won't let that happen," I add.

"The council will stop at nothing to complete their task. There's nowhere in the world she could hide. Now that they know she exists, they won't rest until she's dead."

"Maybe if they meet her and see that she's not like the immortal children of history, they'll feel differently."

He huffs a laugh. "They're not open-minded."

"Tell me about the council. Who put them in charge?"

He ruffles his hair, making it stick out on the sides. "They're a group of five of the most powerful vampires in the world. Four of them have been on the council since before I was a vampire. The newest member has held his seat for around five hundred years."

"Holy shit. They sound like a bunch of old farts."

"They represent the most powerful families and are the absolute law when it comes to vampires." He pauses. "Before the council, there was chaos. I've heard stories throughout the years of vampire clans taking out an entire village or, in some cases, a country. Once the council was enacted, that stopped, and vampires were able to live among humans easily."

"Is Hypatia on the council?"

Viktor looks down. "Yes."

"How old is she?"

"I don't know. She's never told me, but there were rumors of her existence when I was a child. Those rumors were centuries old, maybe more."

I laugh. "It's hard to believe that the teenager driving a bright pink beetle is an ancient vampire of unknown age."

"Don't let her looks deceive you. She may look young and innocent, but she's far from it. She's lethal."

"Does she talk to you like Celeste talks to me?"

"Yes, but I can count on one hand the number of times she's actually done it."

"Did she do it this morning?" I ask, remembering the silent exchange that seemed to happen about his clothing choice earlier.

"Yes." He pulls his cell phone from his pocket, reads a text, and rolls his eyes.

"What?"

"Phillipe and Erick are on their way over." The doorbell rings the moment the words leave his lips.

I open the door to see the two vampires leaning against a post on the porch. "Amelia!" Erick says, taking my hand into his. "You look especially ravishing this evening." He kisses the back of my hand, covering my body in chill bumps.

"Erick! You look as handsome as I remember." I look away from the middle-aged dark-skinned vampire toward the tall younger man behind him. "Phillipe, it's good to see you again. How may I help you, gentlemen?"

"We're here to meet with you and Viktor," Phillipe answers. "I hope we're not imposing."

"Of course not." Viktor is at my side, reeking with charm. "What can we do for you this evening?"

"May we come inside?" Phillipe asks.

"Certainly." Viktor opens the front door wide enough for both of them to enter. They each find a spot to sit before Erick interrupts the silence.

"I'm sure you've heard the rumors of an ancient vampire being in the city."

"I have."

"We believe they're a member of the council." Phillipe sighs. "What we don't know is why they're here.

"Probably related to the cult," I add.

"That's what I think, too, my dear," Erick answers. "Phillipe isn't in agreement." Erick's accent reminds me of warm milk, as his words roll off of his tongue. "Their local leader was most likely just one of many."

"You're right, I don't agree," Phillipe adds. "A human cult isn't of concern to the vampire council. Their concern has always been that of vampires." He turns toward Viktor. "I believe the council is here because of your daughter."

"What would bring you to think that?" Viktor asks, already knowing the answer.

Phillipe walks toward the open fireplace. "Because she's an immortal child, Viktor. You had to know it was only a matter of time before word of her existence would be discovered."

In an instant, Viktor changes from a warm, welcoming friend to something I haven't seen for a while. He's in vampire mode, and I consciously take a step backward. "Phillipe, remember your place. My daughter is none of your concern." He moves closer. "The council will never get their hands on her. She is an innocent victim in all of this."

Erick steps between the two vampires. "Viktor, I don't think Phillipe was threatening Celeste. Possibly you misunderstood. He's simply stating the facts. The council isn't concerned with human affairs. What they are concerned with are ancient traditions and rules. No matter how perfect your child is, the fact remains that she is an immortal child and, therefore, is subject to the rules and regulations as such."

"Get. Out." Viktor is breathing harder than normal and working to control his anger.

"Amelia! Tell them to stop. This isn't necessary." Celeste's voice rings through my mind.

"Stop!" I yell toward the trio. "Celeste says this isn't necessary." The men stop and turn toward me.

"Is she talking to you through your bond, love?" Erick asks, stepping closer.

"Yes." My breaths are short and quick as I wait for her to continue.

"What is she saying?" Viktor asks, relaxing his stance.

I hold up a hand, stopping him from talking. *"Tell them I have a solution to the problem."*

"A solution to what problem?" I ask.

"The immortal child problem. I've found something that will help me grow."

"Celeste, this doesn't make sense."

"Tell them!" she shouts through my mind.

"She says she's found something that will help her grow," I announce.

Viktor looks as confused as I feel. "Help her grow? That's impossible. What is she talking about?"

"Celeste, they want to know what you're talking about." I'm met with silence. *"Celeste?"*

"She's not answering me."

"Dammit." Viktor turns, walking away from the group.

"Tell Daddy not to worry. I'm fine and will be home as soon as I can."

"She says not to worry. That she's fine and will be home soon."

"What is she up to?" he asks, wiping a tear.

"I don't know, but she's a genius. If anyone can figure something like this out, she can."

Erick steps away from the group. "I've heard rumors of such things."

"Tell me everything you know." Viktor's tone leaves no room for argument.

"May I?" Erick motions toward the couch. Viktor nods, following him to the seat. "I've only heard tales and rumors. Nothing definite." He looks down. "A few decades back, I spent some time in the Caribbean. While there, I made friends with some of the local practitioners."

"Voodoo?" I ask.

"Something like that." He smiles. "Through them, I heard stories of children who were forced to grow."

"Do you think that's where she is?" Viktor asks me.

I sit next to Erick. "I think Celeste would do anything to not be trapped in a toddler's body any longer than needed. If there's a possibility she can do something about it, she's not going to stop until she finds it. The Caribbean is one of many options."

"What are we waiting on?" Viktor pulls his phone from his pocket, stepping out of the room to make a call.

"The ancient is a teenage girl named, Hypatia." Both men stare at me like I've just made something up.

"Hypatia is the council member?" Phillipe asks.

"You've heard of her?"

"Yes. She's more powerful than them all."

I picture her driving the bright pink beetle and laugh loudly. "You're joking, right?"

"No, love. Hypatia is the strongest vampire in existence," Erick answers.

"The plane will be at the airport in an hour," Viktor

announces, coming back into the room. "Pack your bags, we're going to Haiti."

......

The conclusion to Amelia's story, "Garden of Discovery and Love" is scheduled for the end of January. Pre-order now to ensure delivery on that day!

GARDEN
OF · DISCOVERY &
LOVE

VAMPIRES OF NEW ORLEANS
BOOK 3

MADALYN RAE

about the author

Madalyn Rae is the pen name for an author who loves telling a story. As a teacher of tiny humans during the day and author by night, she hopes she's able to draw you into her world of fantasy, make-believe, and love, even for a brief moment.

She lives on the Gulf Coast's beautiful white, sandy beaches, with her husband and two loyal, yet mildly obnoxious dogs, Whiskey and Tippi. She's the mother of two amazing adult children and a brand new son-in-law.

When not teaching or pretending to write, Madalyn is immersed in the world of music. Whether playing an instrument or singing a song, she is privileged to know that music is the true magic of the universe.

also by madalyn rae

The Elementals Series

Birth of the Phoenix-Adria's Novella-Prequel

Phoenix of the Sea- Elementals Book 1

Guardian of the Sea- Murphy's Novella

Ashes of the Wind-Elementals Book 2

Embers of the Flame-Keegan's Novella

Fire of the Sky-Elementals Book 3

Salt of the Earth-Elementals Spin-off

Spring 2024

Vampires of New Orleans Series

Garden of the Past-Prequel Novella

Garden of Secret and Shadow-Book 1

Garden of Mystery and Intrigue -Book 2

Garden of Discovery and Love- Book 3

Ravenwood- VONO Spin-off

Spring 2024

Morally Gray Novella Series

Full Moon Christmas

Nipping at Your Nose

Printed in Great Britain
by Amazon

35778506R00171